FICTION HOUSE PRESS
PRESENTS

IMAGINATION
Stories of
Science and Fantasy

December 1950
Vol. 1, No. 2

This reprint edition is a facsimile of the original pulp magazine.
Variations in printing and quality can be attributed to the original magazine which was printed on rough woodpulp paper.
No attempt has been made to politically correct any language deemed inappropriate to the modern reader.

ISBN 978-1-64720-393-1

www.FictionHousePress.com
fictionhousepress@gmail.com

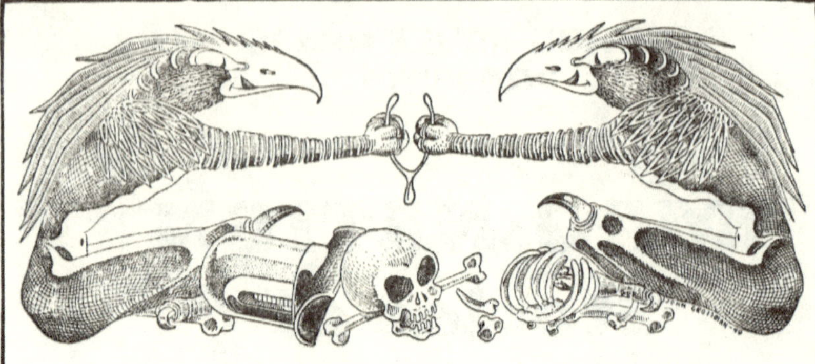

JUST WHAT YOU WERE WISHING FOR!

An original, never-before-published science-fantasy novel of the calibre of the great classics of Merritt, Taine, Wells. . . . A book of satisfying length (116,000 words!) available nowhere else, told with the gripping realism and brilliance of another Poe! A literary "nova" in the science fiction heavens.

The Most Exciting Book Since Merritt's "MOON POOL"

A few of the book's chapter headings will give you some idea of the tremendous scope of the story: Trail Of The Wizard; Votaries Of Ys; Darla Of The Sea-Green Eyes; City Of The Sorcerers; Captives Of The Great Dimension; The Seven Sisters Of Light; The Morning After Eternity; The White Archdruid; In The Grotto Of The Lizard; Vor And The Onyx Key; The Place Of Thunders; The Black Tower . . . twenty-six great chapters in all!

Price $3.50—352 Pages; Cloth Bound; Jacket by Hannes Bok

KINSMEN OF THE DRAGON

By STANLEY MULLEN

SHASTA PUBLISHERS, 5525 S BLACKSTONE, CHICAGO 37, ILLINOIS

Gentlemen: I enclose $3.50 check .... money order .... cash........

Send KINSMEN OF THE DRAGON by return mail, prepaid, to:

NAME ....

ADDRESS ....

CITY .... ZONE........ STATE..................

TABLE OF CONTENTS

DECEMBER 1950

VOLUME 1 NUMBER 2

FEBRUARY ISSUE ON SALE DECEMBER 1

STORIES

FEATURES

Front cover painting by Harold McCauley illustrating "Meet Me In Tomorrow"

Published bi-monthly by Clark Publishing Company, at 1144 Ashland Avenue, Evanston, Illinois. Second-class entry applied for at the Post Office, Evanston, Illinois. Application for additional entry at Sandusky, Ohio, is pending.

FROM the fan mail that has already poured in, as this editorial is written for a deadline on the second issue, it is quite apparent that IMAGINATION has met with your enthusiastic approval. That makes us very happy and proud. It proves a big point to us. That you wanted a magazine of this type—a magazine with what one of the fan letters called "class," and others, "darned entertaining stories!"

WELL, whether or not we have that certain "class" that some of the readers have mentioned, we do agree with the latter viewpoint about entertaining stories. After all, you can have all the class in the world, be a great success insofar as quality is concerned, but if you don't have "darned entertaining stories" you just won't survive. So you can count on a lot of entertainment in IMAGINATION. If you get quality along with it, and maybe some of that "class" appeal, we're sure you won't mind—and neither will we. As long as we're both entertained—you and we—we can't go wrong. It's as simple as that.

NOW take this issue. We don't mean to go prating about the stories, for you're going to be reading them yourself in a few minutes. But we would like to call your attention to just a few of them. Not the stories so much, as the authors.

FIRST of all there's a newcomer to the science-fantasy field. His name is Harold (Hal) Annas, and he hails from Suffolk, Virginia. We found a manuscript in the mails one day. Just an ordinary looking manuscript—one of a hundred that arrived at the same time. We didn't recognize the name of the author, but of course that didn't bother us since you never know when you're going to find a new Heinlein, Bradbury, or Rog Phillips, all three men top names in their field. So we started to read THE ULTIMATE QUEST. And we started to laugh almost at the same time. Real chuckles, the kind that tickle your ribs with solid humor. We kept chuckling all the way through the story, and when we got to the end we knew that we had made a find. Hal Annas got his first check with that story, and while you have never heard of him before, we predict you'll hear quite a lot of him in the future. He has a refreshingly new style to add to the field. His story is not heavy on the "plot" side. Rather, it is a satire on man and his sophisticated world. The big thing is that it will give you a few laughs. That's entertainment. And any writer who can entertain a reader won't have to worry about a future market for his fiction. . . . As a matter of fact, we bought a new story from Hal Annas just the other day. All we'll say right now is that it's even better than the one in this issue! So that's our introduction to you of a newcomer we're happy to have discovered. It should happen every day!

AS long as we're on the subject of newcomers, we can't neglect to mention another new writer to the field who has a story featured in this issue of "Madge." We didn't buy the first story of Betsy Curtis. We understand that Tony Boucher of THE MAGAZINE OF FANTASY & SCIENCE FICTION had that honor. But we do know that we bought a story from Miss Curtis before her first one saw print in Tony's book, so we were right in there picking talent along with our worthy colleague.

MISS Curtis, who resides in Canton, New York, writes with an amazing clarity and depth. Her work is on the serious side, in contrast to Hal Annas, and we feel that she should go a long way in the field. She has that rare gift of being able to "project" the reader into her story, making him feel it as reality, rather than as escapism. But you'll know just what we mean after you finish reading THE OLD ONES.

ONE thing we're going to try and do with all issues of "Madge" from here on in. That's present a balanced diet of stories—some on the serious side, some in a humorous vein, some with a lot of solid action adventure, and maybe here and there a yarn that will make you stop and think. We know that every reader has a certain taste he wants satisfied, so we're going to please everybody. You'll like all the yarns we present, in one way or another, but you'll find some of them slanted especially for you. And by "you" we mean singularly and all inclusive. As we see it, that's about the best policy, if you wish to call it that, that a magazine could adopt.

YOU'LL remember last issue we talked about stories in which the realism of the future would play a great part. We've got some really top-notch fiction coming up in future issues that will bear this out in more detail.

BUT enough of stories for the present. We'd like to talk a bit more about covers right now. And in particular, about the coming cover on the third issue, which will go on sale on December 1st. If you recall, we told you you'd find some interesting artwork in forthcoming issues of "Madge," and we think the third issue will bear this out. It features an interplanetary cover by Malcolm Smith, who is without question the leading cover artist in this particular type. But it's not an ordinary interplanetary scene. It's one that will hit your eye with a dramatic impact. Actually, we can't think of a way of describing it adequately, it's that good. And perhaps we're not being strictly fair in even talking about it for all we can do is arouse your curiosity without satisfying it. But when you get your copy on December 1st we're sure you'll be pleased with it. So on that happy note we'll let you get down to reading the current issue. Let us know how you like it. . . . Rap.

Andy stood out in the small clearing, waving a goodbye to them, while behind him a strange metallic globe suddenly shimmered in the air . . .

MEET ME IN TOMORROW

By GUY ARCHETTE

Ellen was everything Andy Pearce wanted in a girl. Yet he could never let her know of his love, for she was part of a world he was about to leave!

THE gravel road wound its way through quiet country fields cloaked in the fresh green of early summer. Andy Pearce watched it with expectant eyes and the odd feeling that it was winding up within him like twine, making an ever-growing ball of tension.

It wouldn't be long now, he thought. He was excited—and not

a little afraid.

Abruptly Pearce leaned toward the windshield of the coupe. "That's the place, Dave!" He pointed to a wall of trees that had just come into view around a curve.

"At last!" Ellen Thorpe sighed, from her seat between the two men. "I was beginning to think it would take all day to reach this wonderful picnic spot of yours, Andy."

"It better be good," Dave Fuller growled. "After letting myself be coaxed into this trip and driving all morning."

"Good?" Pearce was grinning, though his voice held no humor. "Dave, I guarantee it's going to be better than anything you can possibly imagine."

Ellen frowned at Pearce. "You know, Andy, somehow you scare me."

"It's the beast in him," Fuller put in. "The gals are always fooled by Andy's curly hair and soulful eyes, but sooner or later they wake up to his true nature."

She wrinkled her nose at him. "I think you're a beast, too. All men are beasts. But as for Andy, he takes first prize. He had to go and ruin the date I made for him and Susie. It practically broke her heart that she wasn't going with us today."

Pearce moved his hands in a helpless gesture. "I'm sorry about Susie, but this was one time I didn't want to be fixed up with a date."

"I don't think you ever did," Ellen said bitterly. "I practically had to browbeat you into all the dates I made for you."

"Your concern for my . . . well, call it social life, is deeply appreciated," Pearce returned with mild sarcasm.

"Yours?" she protested. "Andy Pearce, I assure you that arranging your dates was nothing more or less than self-defense on my part. I didn't want people to get the idea that I was preparing for a life of bigamy by always going out with two men."

"I plead self-defense, too." Pearce was sober. "Romantic complications are something I wanted to avoid. Anyhow, getting back to this picnic today, I wanted it to be strictly a family affair."

Fuller's red head swung around in dismay. "Good grief, Andy, don't tell me all your relatives are going to be out here! If that's the reason you wanted to visit your boyhood stamping grounds——"

"Relax," Pearce said. "No relatives. I was speaking figuratively. I never had enough relatives to mention. An uncle brought me up, and he departed this vale of tears a long time ago."

Fuller looked relieved. "Relatives make me nervous."

"Then you'd better stop this rattle-trap of yours," Pearce gestured at the trees, now almost abreast of the coupe. "Not that the fact we've arrived has anything to do with it."

FULLER turned the car into a stretch of grass beside the road and braked to a stop. "End of the line!" he announced. Then he glanced at Pearce in uneasy speculation. "Or is it? I hope it doesn't take a stiff hike to get to your boyhood Eden."

"Quit griping," Pearce said. "We're almost there now. And don't forget I promised that this is going to be worth your trouble."

"I'll bet!" Fuller muttered. Despite his skeptical tone, his blue eyes lingered on Pearce in veiled wonder.

Pearce let himself stiffly out of the car. Ellen followed, glancing about her curiously. She was a slim, graceful girl, dark, yet with a quality of glowing vividness. Her shining hair had been cut short in the current fashion, its boyish effect offset by her large, lustrous eyes and full red lips.

She stretched on tiptoe, for a moment standing motionless and statuesque. Pearce watched her with a sudden, flashing intensity. Pain touched him, and regret.

But it was too late—too late even to think of what might have been . . .

She turned. "This is a wild, lonely-looking place you've dragged us out to, Andy."

He nodded, his gray eyes kindling with memories. "It hasn't changed since I was a kid. Except for the road. It's got gravel on it now."

"What, no red carpet?" Fuller asked in mock surprise, as he too emerged from the coupe. "A lousy welcome for our boy Andy. No red carpet."

"Cut it out," Ellen admonished. "These aren't the surroundings for low comedy. Let's just be simple, sociable folk enjoying a picnic. Bring out the eats, and we'll get started."

Looking exaggeratedly chastened, Fuller opened the trunk at the rear of the coupe and began handing out objects. There was a basket of food, blankets, a record player, and a cardboard carton containing beer packed in dry ice. There was also a large suitcase belonging to Pearce.

Fuller hefted this exploratively. "Just a little something for the picnic," he said, glancing at Ellen. "That's what Andy told me when he put this hunk of luggage in the car. Why, it's as heavy as the national debt!"

"Nobody's asking you to carry it," Pearce said mildly.

"No—but I wish I could figure out what you're up to," Fuller returned.

Pearce shook a warning finger. "If wishes were limousines, the accident toll among joy-riding beggars would be terrific."

"Very funny." Fuller turned to Ellen again. "Do you think it's decent of Andy to worry his friends like this?"

She studied Pearce a moment, her dark eyes solemn. Then she

moved her slim shoulders in a philosophical shrug. "Since we've come this far, I guess we'll just have to put up with it."

"That's the spirit!" Pearce said. "Just put your lives in my hands, little ones—and let the insurance premiums fall where they may." He bent to pick up the suitcase and the record player, hoping that he had moved quickly enough to hide the pain and unhappiness that had momentarily showed in his face. The situation was proving more difficult than he had thought it would be. He had hoped to make the picnic a light-hearted affair, to keep Fuller and Ellen from suspecting at the very outset that something unusual was taking place.

HE strode into the woods. Fuller followed with the blankets and the beer carton, and Ellen with the basket of food.

The glade proved easy enough to locate. It was smaller than Pearce remembered, but the semi-circle of large stones along one side was much the same. The trees that rose all around gave their old effect of seclusion, of shutting out the world. Beyond the enclosure they made were the shadows cast by interlaced boughs, and through these came the plaintive cries of birds, somehow like the sound of waves on an island shore.

Pearce glanced around him slowly, relishing the familiarity of the scene, his thoughts leaping a chasm of fifteen years. One memory in particular was suddenly very vivid.

"So this is the place, Andy," Ellen said behind him. "Why, it's just perfect!" She swung to Fuller. "Don't you think this is worth the drive?"

"I refuse to give my opinion until I've had enough beer to put me in the proper mood," Fuller growled.

"Start opening it, then," Ellen said. "I'll get the food ready."

They ate seated on the blankets, around the appetizingly laden tablecloth Ellen had spread. Pearce was too intense to have much of an interest in food, but he managed to consume what normally would have been expected of him. He was sharply aware that the minutes were running out, that the deadline was now swiftly approaching. The knowledge strengthened the undercurrent of dread within him, brought a pang of sadness.

But he did not want these last moments with Ellen and Dave to be touched with melancholy, nor did he want them to sense his troubled emotional state. He helped to keep a casual conversation going, and whenever this threatened to lag, he started the record player.

Shadows deepened within the glade as the afternoon wore on. Pearce helped Ellen to clean up the picnic remains, then sprawled beside Fuller to finish what was left of the beer. From the record player came the strains of a symphony. Ellen seated herself nearby, tapping one slender foot in time to the music.

Distractedly Pearce thought of the fleeting, precious minutes. He glanced at his watch.

Fuller abruptly sat up. "There you go again, Andy!"

"What?" Pearce was startled.

"Looking at that doggoned watch of yours." Fuller's expression was accusing. "You aren't fooling anybody, Andy. You're up to some thing—and it's about time you explained yourself. This beating around the bush is no way to treat your friends. You drag us out here, to the place where you grew up. You have a suitcase along that certainly doesn't have bricks in it. You drop mysterious hints about something special."

Fuller's voice softened, his blue eyes turned anxious. "Just what have you got up your sleeve, Andy?"

PEARCE looked away, pain, a sudden tightness in his chest. He said slowly, "Well, I'm taking a sort of trip, Dave. I . . . I'm afraid I'm never going to see you and Ellen again."

"Andy!" Ellen's voice was a stricken whisper.

"Never see us again . . . " Fuller muttered blankly.

The symphony came to an end. There was a moment of strained quiet.

"What are you talking about, Andy?" Fuller demanded in hurt bewilderment. "Where are you going that you'll never see me and Ellen again?"

"It's a long story," Pearce said. He grinned faintly. "I mean that. It's a story that begins fifteen years in the past and ends some two-thousand years in the future."

Fuller and Ellen were rigid, staring. Pearce drained the last of his beer and lighted a cigarette.

"In another way," he went on, "the story really begins right where we are now. This part of the woods always was a favorite spot of mine. I'd sneak off here to read books and magazines that I borrowed from a neighbor whose taste in literature was on the blood and thunder side—lucky for me. My uncle didn't like to see me reading, thought it a waste of time. But it was in the middle of the Depression, and there wasn't much else to do. Uncle was an intolerant old bird, a widower, and he wasn't happy about getting stuck with me. I didn't like it, either, but there didn't seem anything a twelve-year-old kid could do about it."

Pearce drew at his cigarette, his gray eyes squinting into distance. "Uncle's chicken farm was a lonely place, and in self-defense I guess I developed a lot more imagination than most kids my age. Most of the time I wasn't on the farm at all—except when Uncle gave me a spanking by way of a reminder. I was out on the deserts of Mars, or walking the streets of a lost city in Africa, or tracking down an international spy ring in London. This day-dreaming, as I can see now, was pretty important."

Fuller said impatiently, "But Andy, what on earth does this build-up have to do with the trip you're going to make?"

"Keep your shirt on," Pearce said. "You'll see."

He resumed. "What I've outlined was the general situation when I came here one summer afternoon, to read a book. About a half-hour later something happened that practically made me jump out of my skin. The air in the glade seemed suddenly to thicken, and the trees all around grew crazily twisted, as though seen through optical glass. I felt oddly light, dizzy and sick at the same time. And from somewhere came a deep, humming sound—the kind of sound that might have been made by a string on a giant harp.

"The next thing I knew there was a sort of machine in the glade that seemed to have popped right out of nowhere. It was a metal globe about eight feet across, with tapering legs or supports on the bottom to keep it upright. There was the outline of a door in the side turned toward me.

"I was scared stiff, of course, but I had been reading about this kind of thing happening in stories — and as far as I was concerned, there was hardly any dividing line between stories and real life. So I stayed put. I knew the machine was something special, because I'd never seen anything like it outside of the illustrations in the more imaginative type of magazines."

PEARCE drew at his cigarette again. Fuller and Ellen were like store window figures, arranged in attitudes of rapt attention.

"After several seconds the door in the side of the machine opened and a woman stepped out. I thought she was the most beautiful creature I had ever seen, a princess—or an angel. She looked the way ancient Egyptian women must have looked. She made me think of a tropical flower, which wasn't far from truth, considering that she came from a time when the Earth was—or will be—a great deal warmer than it is now. She was wearing a sort of thin dress that sparkled as though covered with jewels, and over this she held a long cloak. It was summer, but I suppose it was a bit too cool for her.

"She smiled at me—and I was glad I had stuck around. She said she hoped I hadn't been frightened by the appearance of her machine, and I guess I tried to sell her the idea that I strangled lions with my bare hands just for exercise. Then she explained that her name was Nela, and that she had come from two-thousand years in the future especially to see me. Her machine, of course, was a time machine."

"Good grief!" Fuller said explosively. "What kind of a gag are you trying to put over, Andy?"

"I know just how it all sounds," Pearce returned. "But believe me, for one of the few times in my life I'm dead serious. Keep quiet and listen. I don't have much time left."

"Go on, Andy," Ellen said. "I'm fascinated."

Pearce took a final puff of his cigarette, crushed it out in the grass, and continued. "Nela explained how it was possible to travel in time, but in the sort of terms a kid would understand. Even what I've figured out up to now isn't specific enough to be worth detailing, except to say that what we consider space and time are merely illusions of sense perception. They are really one stationary system or complex — stationary, yet dynamic and changing within itself—and under certain conditions one can travel through this system, from future to past, or the other way around, like through a museum — the biggest museum that can possibly be imagined.

"Nela's machine operated on energy principles that won't be known for a great many years yet, and it will be even longer before those principles are put into application. She was, in effect, making a round-trip from one part of the museum to another—a trip that took her across two thousand years of what we call time, or across a couple of hundred light years of what we call space. It's one and the same thing. Actually, she was following a sort of huge orbit, and was, so to speak, stopping off along the route. A trip between one point and another can be made only once, because even that one trip brings changes which affect the whole system, or complex. One point, it seems, is always shifted so that it lies outside of any orbit which can be plotted from the other.

"Nela told me about the kind of world she came from, too, and it sounded—and still sounds—like a perfect place. There was, so she said, practically no government, practically no laws, restrictions, or penalties. In two thousand years enough had been learned about the mind to make these unnecessary. Men at last were truly equal. There was no longer any need to work for a living. Machines of all sorts attended to every task and human requirement. Earth was one huge garden—and there was plenty of room for everyone. Men had reached the stars and had found new homes almost beyond number.

"An ideal picture—but there was a catch to it. The machines on which Nela's people depended were breaking down, and it seemed nobody knew even how to begin repairing them. The men of her time could take suns apart and put them back together again, but the machines baffled them in much the same way that our atomic scientists would be baffled when it came to repairing a suit of Medieval armor. The answer to the problem was to obtain the help of persons who understood the construction and operation of the machines at least as well as Medieval armorers understood their steel suits. And that answer — in both cases—lay back in time."

PEARCE changed position on the blanket under him and glanced at his watch. He went on, "Time travel had been accomplished well before Nela's period, but the process had proved too involved and tricky for serious, large-scale use. The important thing, though, was that a number of machines were immediately available for time travel, and Nela was one of those chosen to operate them. She was, it seems, a gal of parts. In addition to being one of the leaders of a world-wide group which had been formed to deal with the machine break-down problem, she was also an expert on time travel and an authority on Twentieth Century life.

"Actually, you see, Nela's people were undergoing a cultural renaissance, a reawakening of interest in every field of knowledge and endeavor. For many hundreds of years there had been stagnation. The machines had filled every human want, and there had been little need for effort of any kind. Also, progress had been discouraged by a hidebound government, which had remained in power through its control of certain of the more important machines. The government had fallen when realization came that it could do nothing to keep the machines in repair, but the damage had been done. After centuries of a hands-off attitude toward the machines, nobody else knew how to repair them, either. Rapid progress was made everywhere except in this one direction.

"Nela and the others decided to travel to different points in time and obtain specialists who would each be able to deal with some particular repair job on the machines. The machines, of course, were not the product of any one time period, but were the cumulative result of the knowledge and skills of different periods. I was the specialist with whom contact was made at this point in time. It was, I realize now, quite a complicated business.

"When a beautiful girl appears in a time machine and tells some young man she needs his help, he doesn't just drop whatever he happens to be doing and go sailing blithely off into the mysterious future. Not in real life. He has to consider his family and friends, the career he was working on, all the things familiar and important to him, his surroundings, interests and amusements, climate, customs, clothing—all the rest. He has to consider that he might not be happy in the future, that he might not fit, that he might not even be physically comfortable, that the beautiful girl herself might very well turn out to be disappointing.

"But if he is a young man of average intelligence, he most likely wouldn't even bother to consider these things. He simply would refuse to believe the beautiful girl from the future, would be certain it was some sort of a hoax. Or he might even be scared stiff by the very idea of traveling in time. All of which boils down to the fact that the girl from the future would face a mighty tough job getting the right kind of young man to help her."

"I get it now," Fuller broke in musingly. "So that's what your suitcase is for, Andy." Then his voice sharpened with protest. "But it . . . it's ridiculous! I just can't believe it's possible."

"The young man of average intelligence speaking," Pearce murmured."

"Yeah?" Fuller swung to Ellen. "What do you think?"

SHE shook her dark head slightly, lower lip caught between her teeth. "I'm trying not to think . . . Go on, Andy—before I start thinking."

"Hate to have that happen, if Dave's mental acrobatics are any example." Pearce abruptly sobered, glancing at his watch. "Well," he resumed, "Nela and the others foresaw the difficulties they would encounter in obtaining help, and they figured out what they hoped would be a fool-proof method of approach. What happened in my case shows what this was. It seems Nela first scouted out a group of specialists to find a couple with the right qualifications. The man she wanted had to be young and adventurous, without any family or romantic ties. Then she narrowed her field still further by tracing her selection back to childhood and making direct contact there.

"It was clever—for after all, the child is father to the man. A child is credulous and imaginative to an extent a man is not. And a child is adventurous, will let his enthusiasms carry him spontaneously where a man will hesitate and look for a catch. Most of all a child is impressionable and can be imbued with an idea which he will follow like a beacon light all his life.

"I was the child Nela finally settled on. The Andy Pearce she had first scouted still existed in time, and nothing would change for him. But no paradox is involved, for what we call time is an illusion, a subjective quality arising from an awareness of objective conditions—and these conditions are not quite what we think they are. That first Andy Pearce was something like a bubble moving in a glass tube. All Nela did was put another bubble in motion. The tube itself was not affected, nor was time shifted, bent, nullified, or anything of the sort. Each bubble was as real as anything can be said to be real, each existed in its own particular space-time, each was completely distinct and independent of the other.

"Nela visited me here several times, while she told me all the details of her mission. She was also getting acquainted with me and giving me time to thoroughly digest the idea of going with her. I agreed to go, of course. It seemed the most natural thing in the world to do, and I didn't change my mind. Once she had satisfied herself on that score, she worked out a plan of operations for me to follow until I was finally ready to leave. The plan took in schools, subjects, finances, and the like. Nela, you see, was making a big improvement on the first Andy Pearce.

"I never saw Nela again after those first visits. It was quite unnecessary, as I can see now. For she and her people understood the mind with an amazing thoroughness, and during her talks she subtly injected me with knowledge, emotions and ideals that set me in motion toward my goal as effectively and undeviatingly as though I had been hypnotized. And I suspect that she set other bubbles in motion as well, to guide and assist me and generally keep me moving in one direction."

PEARCE gestured. "I've kept moving, all right. Fifteen years have passed, and I know all I need to know about the particular technical subject Nela chose me to handle. I'm ready to leave—and I'm leaving very soon. Nela is coming here to pick me up, having meanwhile been moving to this point along her orbit to make one last stop-off before completing the swing back to her own point in time. There can be no return, for once I leave, this point in time can never be reached again. But then I've had fifteen years to get used to the idea.

"This picnic today was in the nature of a farewell party. You, Dave and Ellen, have been the only friends I've allowed myself — and you've both been fine friends. I wanted you both to know exactly where I was going instead of doing a mysterious fade-out. I felt I owed you that much. I've never told anyone about Nela before—not because the information was likely to prove harmful, or anything of the sort, but simply because it would have created doubts about my sanity. I know I can trust you with it for the same reason."

Pearce spread his hands, grinning crookedly. "Well, I hope that leaves me and my suitcase explained to the complete satisfaction of everyone."

Fuller ran his hand through his red hair in agitation and rose to his feet. "It's the damnedest story I've ever heard, Andy. I wish I could be dead certain it isn't a gag. I can't believe it—or maybe it's just that I can't accept the idea of never seeing you again. If this hadn't come all of a sudden——" He broke off, gesturing helplessly.

"Picnics," Ellen muttered to no one in particular, "are going to be permanently spoiled for me."

"Hell!" Fuller growled. "I need a drink. I guess we all need a drink." He reached out as though to detain Pearce. "Andy, I've got a bottle in the car. For emergencies, you know—and this certainly is an emergency. So stay right here, Andy. Don't go running off into the future until I get back. Promise?"

"On my word of honor," Pearce said.

"Don't drop that bottle, Dave," Ellen put in.

With a last anxious glance at Pearce, Fuller turned and hurried away through the trees. Pearce was abruptly, sharply aware that he was alone with Ellen.

She seemed aware of it also. For a moment her dark eyes met his with a kind of pensive directness, then dropped.

There was an uncomfortable silence.

"I'll never be quite the same again after today, Andy," Ellen murmured at last.

He stared morosely at his hands. "I'm sorry. I guess I did spring the story a bit too suddenly. Maybe I shouldn't have said anything at all, done a quiet fade-out."

"I think I'd rather have known what happened to you than otherwise." She traced a design on the blanket with one slim finger, then said, "Andy, you made a remark in the car—about avoiding what you called romantic complications. Were you avoiding them because you were eventually going away with this Nela female?"

He nodded. "Something like that."

"Wasn't it because you were in love with her?"

"Why, I . . . I don't think so." He was startled. "I guess it's true that I had a crush on her as a kid, but I haven't seen her for fifteen years. I hardly feel I ever knew her."

"Then even though you're going away with her, there is someone you care for?"

He hesitated for an aching instant, finally managed a shrug. "It isn't important. Not any more."

"It is—to me. Andy, this is no time for historical novel gallantry or radio soap opera self-renunciation. This is the last chance we'll ever have to be completely frank with each other." Her dark eyes were intent. "Andy, do you love me?"

"I . . . well—" He groped in confusion, with the feeling that he had suddenly found himself on a tight-rope, hundreds of feet in the air. Then he nodded miserably. "Yes."

"Then just why did you take it for granted that I was Dave's girl?" Ellen demanded bitterly.

"I thought Dave was the one you were interested in. He was my best friend, and I didn't want to——"

"You thought! Didn't it ever occur to you to find out?"

HE made a helpless gesture. "I wanted to, Ellen—but I don't see what good it could have done. I was going away, you know."

"Don't you think I could have changed your mind about that? Don't you think I can change your mind — even now?" Abruptly she leaned toward him, her small face lighted as though by some fierce inner fire, at once pleading and demanding. "Andy—kiss me!"

Despite himself, that fire touched him, kindled to a blaze. His lips met hers with a quickening pressure, his hands slipped from her shoulders to draw her tightly against him. For long seconds nothing else had reality or importance. The glade dissolved around him, and he seemed to float in a dark sea that rose and fell with a wild rhythm.

Then awareness of his act exploded in him. He released the girl abruptly and drew away.

"It's hopeless, Ellen! I can't back down now."

She shook her dark head in swift protest. "It isn't hopeless, Andy. It isn't too late. I just proved that to you."

"But Nela is depending on me. I can't let her down."

"You owe her nothing! She took advantage of you at a time when you weren't mature and experienced enough to exercise good judgment. Why should you feel obligated to her now?"

"I agreed to go with her. If I let her down, she won't be able to obtain a replacement with my particular type of training. She can visit this point in time only once."

"That's her problem, Andy. You have your own life to live. Why shouldn't you be able to live it as you choose? You don't know just what sort of a life the future holds for you—but you do know what you'll find here."

He gripped his knees hard, finally shook his head. "This is something bigger than we are, Ellen—something more important than your personal happiness, or mine. It isn't just that Nela is depending on me. Behind her is a whole civilization. It's the greatest responsibility a man can be given. If I backed down, I'd never feel right again. I'd always have it on my conscience."

She slumped in despair. "Then there's nothing else I can do to change your mind?"

"Nothing, Ellen. I'm sorry."

Silence closed down again. A painful, uneasy silence, the silence of people between whom an unsurmountable barrier exists.

The silence added fuel to Pearce's inner turmoil. He wished that it had been possible to leave without hurting Ellen, even without discovering that she returned his own feelings. The knowledge that he would never see her again had been difficult enough to face. For in these last months the picture of her had come to haunt him—Ellen, with her shining dark hair and her slim vital body, at once gaily humorous and warmly sympathetic. He knew that he would never forget her, or cease thinking of the happiness he might have found with her.

"It might be a good idea to wipe that lipstick off your face, Andy," Ellen murmured at last.

Pearce fumbled for a handkerchief and scrubbed at his mouth. The action brought forward something that had been hovering at the back of his mind.

"What about Dave?" he asked abruptly. "I hope I haven't spoiled anything for him."

SHE shook her head with a grave seriousness. "Dave knows how I feel. And it isn't much of a loss where he's concerned, because he's been taking a growing interest in Susie. She has a terrific crush on him, and that's the reason she wanted to come with us so badly today. But you insisted on a three-sided party and as usual left Dave to nursemaid me."

Pearce felt a dull amazement. Engrossed with his preparations for leaving he had not sensed the emotional undercurrents beneath the outwardly placid surface of Dave and Ellen.

Ellen, he thought suddenly. Dave was accounted for—but Ellen? He could not voice the question, feeling himself too inextricably bound up in it.

There was the sound of footsteps as Fuller returned, brandishing a bottle. "Here it is!" he announced. "Get out the glasses, Ellen."

She produced three plastic tumblers from the basket, and Fuller poured a generous drink in each. He raised his own tumbler in a solemn gesture.

"Here's to Andy. Bon voyage—and a high old time in the future!"

"Thanks," Pearce said in self-conscious acknowledgement. He swallowed the whisky in a gulp, felt its raw warmth spread through him.

Bon voyage, he thought. The voyage part was true enough. But he doubted if he would have a high old time. He would always think of Ellen. And Dave. And all the other people he had known, who would continue to move against the old familiar background of their existence, among all the old familiar things, without sudden violent change, or pain, or loss. He would think of movies and dances, baseball games and parties. And restaurants and nightclubs and small quiet bars. And apple pie and coffee, hamburgers and malted milk. And his favorite brand of cigarettes. and two-pants suits and straw hats in the summer. And beer and sport pages and classical records on a drowsy Sunday afternoon. And politics and elections and critical internal situations. And crowded downtown streets and quiet suburban cottages—all the other things he had known and liked, or had taken for granted and had not thought much about. He would think of them because they wouldn't exist in the future any more, because people would have changed, would have different ideals, habits and tastes.

Fuller filled the tumblers again and made an effort at the sort of artificially cheerful small talk that precedes the sailing of a troop ship.

Pearce, who had surreptitiously been keeping check on his watch, finally gestured. "It's almost time for Nela to pick me up—and I'd like to be alone when she comes. The situation might be too complicated if you and Ellen were present, Dave. I want things to be as easy as possible all around."

Fuller looked disappointed. "I was kind of hoping to get a look at this gal from the future, Andy. I still don't know whether to believe your story or not."

"Give me the benefit of the doubt, anyway, will you?" Pearce pleaded. He turned to Ellen. "You'll do this last favor for me?"

She nodded and leaned forward on tiptoe. "Good-bye, Andy—and good luck." Her voice was little more than a whisper.

HE touched her lips with his and for a moment stood looking down at her, thinking once more of what might have been. An echo of his own thoughts seemed to glisten wetly in her dark eyes. Abruptly she turned away.

Pearce gripped Fuller's hand. "So long, Dave."

"Take care of yourself, Andy." Fuller looked painfully reflective, then suddenly held out the bottle. "Here, Andy, you take this. You might need it."

Pearce watched with a deep inward aching as Fuller and Ellen strode from the glade. Reaching the trees, they turned to look back at him. They hesitated, waved—were gone.

Pearce felt that the last door to the past had been irrevocably closed.

He looked down at the bottle he was holding and lifted it to his mouth. Then he lighted a cigarette, glanced at his watch again, and fell to pacing along one edge of the glade. His eyes roved tensely about him, expectant and dreading.

Thoughts shifted uneasily in his mind. Would Nela actually appear? Fifteen years had passed for him—a matter of a few hours to her. But perhaps something had gone wrong. Perhaps she had miscalculated somewhere.

And on mental scales he balanced Ellen against the future, wondering if his choice had been wise. Could the future possibly hold the happiness he might have known with Ellen, in the age familiar to him?

He heard a car motor start up in the distance. The sound rose in volume, then began fading. Dave and Ellen were on their way back to the city.

He felt suddenly alone—somehow abandoned.

Raising the bottle to his lips again, he resumed his nervous pacing. And then he stopped, frozen, aware of a change in his surroundings. The air in the glade was thickening queerly, the trees all around were growing crazily distorted. And he heard a deep humming sound—the kind of sound that might have been made by a string on a giant harp.

Across the glade, appearing as though from nothingness itself, an object was taking shape—a metal globe. Bands of distortion surrounded it like ripples in water. For an instant the globe seemed unsubstantial, illusory—then it was solid, resting quietly on the floor of the glade.

Pearce watched it, his heart pounding.

"Andy!"

The call hit him like a physical blow. Stunned, he whirled to see Ellen hurrying toward him through the trees.

"Andy!" she cried again. "Are you all right?"

"Ellen!" he gasped. "What are you doing here? I thought you left with Dave."

SHE caught breathlessly at his arm, steadying herself. "I made him go without me. I . . . I couldn't leave you, Andy." Her voice rose. "I'm going with you!"

His mind whirled in dismayed confusion. He sent a swift glance at the metal globe. Any moment now, the door would open——

"Ellen, you can't go!"

"Why not? I'm willing to take the risk. And I'll be happy, whatever the future is like, as long as I'm with you."

He shook his head in despair. "It . . . well, I'm afraid it's just impossible, that's all. No provision has been made for you. I don't know even if there would be room for you. I don't know if Nela can allow you in her plans, or——"

He broke off. Glancing at the globe again, he saw that the door was opening.

He waited for Nela to appear, wondering what her reaction would be when she saw Ellen, wondering how this hopelessly tangled situation could possibly be resolved.

The door of the globe stood fully open. Nothing else happened.

Pearce waited a moment longer, puzzled, then slowly looked into the globe. Except for two padded seats and a myriad of instruments on the curving walls, the interior of the machine was empty.

He turned in bewilderment to Ellen. "Something's wrong! Nela isn't inside."

Ellen looked gravely thoughtful. "Andy, I think I know what happened to her. She was an authority on Twentieth Century life, you know. She no doubt had all sorts of records to help her. She could speak the kind of English used here, she understood social customs, the economic situation, knew how to dress and act. What she didn't know, she could pick up by being careful and observing. In short, she could pass as an ordinary Twentieth Century girl, and hardly anyone would guess she was different."

Pearce's bewilderment grew. "What are you getting at?"

"Well, Andy, suppose this Nela wanted to make absolutely sure you'd be happy in the future, that nothing would interfere with your efficiency and general well-being. There was a big job ahead of you, and a lot depended on your particular field of knowledge and type of skill. So to make absolutely sure of you she stopped off along her route back to spend your last several months here with you. It wouldn't be hard for a clever girl like her to get acquainted with you and Dave. And you hadn't seen her for fifteen years, Andy. You wouldn't recognize her easily—especially if she'd had her hair cut short and wore Twentieth Century clothes and make-up."

Pearce stared at her a moment longer, then caught at her arms. "Ellen! You . . . you're Nela!"

She nodded slowly, her smile uncertain and touched with shyness. "I hope you aren't disappointed, Andy, or that you hate me for having tricked you the way I did."

He laughed, a wild delight surging up in him. "Neither," he said. "And I'm going to prove it!"

He proved it to her entire satisfaction. Finally, hand in hand, they turned to the doorway of the globe.

"I suppose you brought the machine here by remote control or something of the sort," Pearce told Nela.

"Yes. I had a special gadget in my purse. The machine was here all along, you see, traveling a few minutes ahead in time."

"And Dave?" he said suddenly. Did you tell him?"

"I told him I was going with you and hinted the reason why. He'll figure it out presently—even if he never completely believes it. Little has really changed for Dave. He'll marry Susie and lead a perfectly normal life."

Pearce halted Nela as she was about to enter the globe. "There's a little custom of this time that I'd like to observe. If you're as much of an authority on Twentieth Century life as you claim, you'll understand."

He gathered her up in his arms and carried her over the threshold. Her smile and then the pressure of her lips indicated that she understood.

The door closed. The trees at the edge of the glade grew crazily distorted, shimmering bands enclosed the globe like ripples in water, there was a humming sound like a giant harp string——

And then the glade was empty.

PERSONALS . . .

Wanted: Socii Stili scribere in lingua Latina de Scientia Fabula et (aut) astrologia vera amateure (non nuntiando fortunarum ab stellis). Scribe ad C. Palmerum Harris, 101 N. Spring Garden Ave., Nutley 10, N. J. . . . Fred Stitt, 2538 Foothill Blvd., La Crescenta, Calif. would like to hear from any rocket enthusiast or experimenter interested in a steady correspondence . . Wanted: out-of-print "Cosmic Forces as They Were Taught in Mu" by Emory H. Mann, RFD, No. 1, West Townsend, Mass . . . Roger Nelson, 1018 Johnson Ave., San Diego 3, Calif. would like to hear from near-by fans who are interested in forming a fan club . . . If you have copies of ASF prior to Dec. '45, Dave Fried, Box 5206, Phoenix, Arizona will pay 50c each for them . . . For sale: A Princess of Mars, Gods of Mars, Warlord of Mars, Swords of Mars, Thuvia, Maid of Mars, Chessmen of Mars, Fighting Man of Mars, Synthetic Men of Mars, Pirates of Venus, The Moon Colony and Beast of the Haitian Hills; $1.00 each. Write Roland Dumontet, 363 Linden Blvd., Brooklyn, NY. . . . Howard DeVore, 16536 Evanston, Detroit 24, Mich. wants Strange Tales, Oriental Stories, Magic Carpet, Miracle Science, Weird Tales prior to '34 and ASF prior to '39 . . . Anyone interested in a solution to economic troubles and world conflicts write Harold Friedrichs, 3933 Canal St., Apt. B, New Orleans, La. . . . Joseph Kinne would like to hear from penpals 14 or 15 years old. Joe's address is 255 S. Sixth Street, Fulton NY. . . . Wanted: Any and all copies of "Unknown Worlds" by L. N. Berkley, 411 University Ave., Ithaca, NY. . . . For sale: American and British Unknowns; AS, '28-'29; FFN, Vol. I, No. 1, 4 and 5; FFM, '39-'42; Weird, '39-'41; Marvel Stories, Super Science, Wonder Quarterly, Thrilling Wonder, Air Wonders; also, The New Adam, by Weinbaum. For complete list and prices Write Charles Baird, 161 Albemarle St., Springfield, Mass. . . . Roger Nelson, 1018 Johnson Ave., San Diego 3, Calif. wants Argosies containing the stories of Farley, Merritt, Cummings and Burroughs . . . Eusifanso, published by the Eugene Science Fantasy Society, 146 E. 12th St., Eugene, Oregon is available for 10c per copy, 6/50c . . . Earl Parris, Box 228, Lewis, Delaware has a supply of science-fiction pins which he is selling for $1.00 each. These pins are triangular with a symbolic design in gold, green and black. For further description and information, write to Earl Parris . . . Challenge, a new fanzine devoted to poetry, is being published by Lilith Lorraine, Stanton A. Coblentz and Evelyn Thorne. Send 30c for one copy or $1.00 for four to Challenge, Rogers, Arkansas . . . James Welch, c/o Wesley Roscoe, Petrolia, Calif. has all 12 issues of the '46 ASF in good condition which he will trade for other issues of ASF prior to 1950 . . . Anyone interested in joining the Tri-State Stfantasy Club is invited to write Frank E. McNamar, Granger, Mo. Frank would also like to locate copies of American Thresherman and Thresherman's Review mags . . . Harold Hostetler, 17, would like to hear from penpals. Harold's address is 43 Third St., Cairnbrook, Penna.

* * *

Illustrated by Bill Terry

TECHNICAL SLIP

By John Beynon

Just as he was about to die he received a chance to live his life over again. It was an oversight of course—with a few complications!

"Prendergast," said the Departmental Director, briskly, "there'll be that Contract XB2832 business arising today. Look after it, will you?"

"Very good, sir."

ROBERT Finnerson lay dying. Two or three times before he had been under the impression that he might be dying. He had been frightened, and blusterously opposed to the idea; but this time it was different, he did not bluster, for he had no doubt that the time had come. Even so, he was still opposed; it was under marked protest that he acknowledged the imminence of the nonsensical arrangement.

It was absurd to die at sixty, anyway, and, as he saw it, it would be even more wasteful to die at eighty. A scheme of things in which the wisdom acquired in living was simply scrapped in this way was, to say the least, grossly inefficient. What did it mean?—That somebody else would now have to go through the process of learning all that life had already taken sixty years to teach him; and then be similarly scrapped in the end. No wonder the race was slow in getting anywhere—if, indeed, it were getting anywhere—with this cat-and-mouse, ten-forward-and-nine-back system.

Lying back on one's pillows and waiting for the end in the quiet, dim room, the whole ground plan of existence appeared to suffer from a basic futility of conception. It was a matter to which some of these illustrious scientists might well pay more attention—only, of course, they were always too busy fiddling with less important matters, until they came to his present pass, when they would find it was too late to do anything about it.

Since his reflections had revolved thus purposelessly, and several times, upon somewhat elliptical orbits, it was not possible for him to determine at what stage of them he became aware that he was no longer alone in the room. The feeling simply grew that there was someone else there, and he turned his head on the pillow to see who it might be. The thin clerkly man whom he found himself regarding, was unknown to him, and yet, somehow, unsurprising.

"Who are you?" Robert Finnerson asked him.

The man did not reply immediately. He looked about Robert's own age, with a face, kindly but undistinguished, beneath hair that had thinned and grayed. His manner was diffident, but the eyes which regarded Robert through modest gold-rimmed spectacles were observant.

"Pray do not be alarmed, Mr. Finnerson," he requested.

"I'm not at all alarmed," Robert told him testily. "I simply asked who you are."

"My name is Prendergast—not, of course, that that matters—."

"Never heard of you. What do you want?" Robert said.

Prendergast told him modestly:

"My employers wish to lay a proposition before you, Mr. Finnerson."

"Too late now for propositions," Robert replied shortly.

"Ah, yes, for most propositions, of course, but I think this one may interest you."

"I don't see how—all right, what is it?"

"Well, Mr. Finnerson, we—that is, my employers—find that you are—er—scheduled for demise on April 20th, 1963. That is, of course, tomorrow."

"INDEED," said Robert calmly, and with a feeling that he should have been more surprised than he felt. "I had come to much the same conclusion myself."

"Quite, sir," agreed the other. "But our information also is that you are opposed to this—er—schedule."

"Indeed!" repeated Mr. Finnererson. "How subtle! If that's all you have to tell me, Mr. Pendlebuss—."

"Prendergast, sir. No, that is just by way of assuring you of our grasp of the situation. We are also aware that you are a man of considerable means, and, well, there's an old saying that 'you can't take it with you', Mr. Finnerson."

Robert Finnerson looked at his visitor more closely.

"Just what are you getting at?" he inquired.

"Simply this, Mr. Finnerson. My firm is in a position to offer a revision of schedule—for a consideration."

Robert was already far enough from his normal for the improbable to have shed its improbability. It did not occur to him to question its possibility. He said:

"What revision—and what consideration?"

"Well, there are several alternative forms," explained Prendergast, "but the one we recommend for your consideration is our Reversion Policy. It is quite our most comprehensive benefit—introduced originally on account of the large numbers of persons in positions similar to yours who were noticed to express the wish 'if only I had my life to live over again'."

"I see," said Robert, and indeed he did. The fact that he had read somewhere or other of legendary bargains of the kind went a long way to disperse the unreality of the situation. "And the catch is?" he added.

Prendergast allowed a trace of disapproval to show.

"The *consideration,"* he said with some slight stress upon the word. "The consideration in respect of a Reversion is a downpayment to us of seventy-five per cent of your present capital."

"Seventy-five per cent! What is this firm of yours?"

Prendergast shook his head.

"You would not recall it, but it is a very old-established concern. We have had—and do have—numbers of notable clients. In the old days we used to work on a basis of—well—I suppose you would call it barter. But with the rise of commerce we changed our methods. We have found it much more convenient to have investable capital than to accumulate souls—especially at their present depressed market value. It is a great improvement in all ways. We benefit considerably, and it costs you nothing but money you must lose anyway—and you are still entitled to call your soul your own; as far, that is, as the law of the land permits. Your heirs will be a trifle disappointed, that's all."

The last was not a consideration to distress Robert Finnerson.

"My heirs are around the house like vultures already," he said. "I don't in the least mind their having a little shock. Let's get down to details, Mr. Snodgrass."

"Prendergast," said the visitor, patiently. "Well now, the usual method of payment is this . . ."

IT was a whim, or what appeared to be a whim, which impelled Mr. Finnerson to visit Sands Square. Many years had passed since he had seen it, and though the thought of a visit had risen from time to time there had seemed never to be the leisure. But now in the convalescence which followed the remarkable, indeed, miraculous recovery which had given such disappointment to his relatives, he found himself for the first time in years with an abundance of spare hours on his hands.

He dismissed the taxi at the corner of the Square, and stood for some minutes surveying the scene with mixed feelings. It was both smaller and shabbier than his memory of it. Smaller, partly because most things seem smaller when revisited after a stretch of years, and partly because the whole of the south side including the house which had been his home was now occupied by an overbearing block of offices: shabbier because the new block emphasized the decrepitude of those Georgian terraces which had survived the bombs and had therefore had to outlast their expected span by twenty or thirty years.

But if most things had shrunk, the trees now freshly in leaf had grown considerably, seeming to crowd the sky with their branches, though there were fewer of them. A change was the bright banks of color from tulips in well tended beds which had grown nothing but tired looking laurels before. Greatest change of all, the garden was no longer forbidden to all but the residents, for the iron railings so long employed in protecting the privileged had gone for scrap in 1941, and never been replaced.

In a recollective mood and with a trace of melancholy, Mr. Finnerson crossed the road and began to stroll again along the once familiar paths. It pleased and yet saddened him to discover the semi-concealed gardener's shed looking just as it had looked fifty years ago. It displeased him to notice the absence of the circular seat which used to surround the trunk of a familiar tree. He wandered on, noting this and remembering that, but in general remembering too much, and beginning to regret that he had come. The garden was pleasant — better looked after than it had been — but, for him, too full of ghosts. Overall there was a sadness of glory lost, with a surrounding shabbiness.

On the east side a well remembered knoll survived. It was, he recalled as he walked slowly up it, improbably reputed to be a last fragment of the earthworks which London had prepared against the threat of Royalist attack.

In the circle of bushes which crowned it, a hard, slatted chair rested in seclusion. The fancy took him to hide in this spot as he had been wont to hide there half a century before. With his handkerchief he dusted away the pigeon droppings and the looser grime. The relief he found in the relaxation of sitting down made him wonder if he had not been overestimating his recuperation. He felt quite unusually weary. . . .

PEACE was splintered by a girl's insistent voice.

"Bobby!" she called. "Master Bobby, where are you?"

Mr. Finnerson was irritated. The voice jarred on him. He tried to disregard it as it called again.

Presently a head appeared among the surrounding bushes. The face was a girl's; above it a bonnet of dark blue straw; around it navy blue ribbons, joining in a bow on the left cheek. It was a pretty face, though at the moment it wore a professional frown.

"Oh, there you are, you naughty boy. Why didn't you answer when I called?"

Mr. Finnerson looked behind him to find the child addressed. There was none. As he turned back he became aware that the chair had gone. He was sitting on the ground, and the bushes seemed taller than he had thought.

"Come along now. You'll be late for your tea," added the girl. She seemed to be looking at Mr. Finnerson himself.

He lowered his eyes, and received a shock. His gaze instead of encountering a length of neatly striped trouser, rested upon blue serge shorts, a chubby knee, white socks and a childish shoe. He waggled his foot, and that in the childish shoe responded. Forgetting everything else in this discovery, he looked down his front at a fawn coat with large, flat brass buttons. At the same moment he became aware that he was viewing everything from beneath the curving brim of a yellow straw hat.

The girl gave a sound of impatience. She pushed through the bushes and emerged as a slender figure in a long, navy blue cape. She bent down. A hand, formalized at the wrist by a stiff cuff, emerged from the folds of the cape and fastened upon his upper arm. He was dragged to his feet.

"Come along now," she repeated. "Don't know what's come over you this afternoon, I'm sure."

Clear of the bushes, she shifted her hold to his hand, and called again.

"Barbara. Come along."

Robert tried not to look. Something always cried out in him as if it had been hurt when he looked at Barbara. But in spite of his will his head turned. He saw the little figure in a white frock turn its head, then it came tearing across the grass looking like a large doll. He stared. He had almost forgotten that she had once been like that: as well able to run as any other child, and forgotten, too, what a pretty, happy little thing she had been.

It was quite the most vivid dream he had ever had. Nothing in it was distorted or absurd. The houses sat with an air of respectability around the quiet square. On all four sides they were of a pattern, with variety only in the colors of the Spring painting that most of them had received. The composite sounds of life about him were in a pattern, too, that he had forgotten; no rising whine of gears, no revving of engines, no squeal of tires; instead, a background with an utterly different cast blended from the clopping of innumerable hooves, light and heavy, and the creak and rattle of carts. Among it was the jingle of chains and bridles, and somewhere in a nearby street a hurdy-gurdy played a once familiar tune. The beds of tulips had vanished, the wooden seat encircled the old tree as before, the spiked railings stood as he remembered them, stoutly preserving the garden's privacy. He would have liked to pause and taste the flavor of it all again, but that was not permissible.

"Don't drag, now," admonished the voice above him. "We're late for your tea now, and Cook won't like it."

There was a pause while she unlocked the gate and let them out. Then with their hands in hers they crossed the road toward a familiar front door, magnificent with new shiny green paint and bright brass knocker. It was a little disconcerting to find that their way in lay by the basement steps and not through this impressive portal.

IN the nursery everything was just as it had been, and he stared around him, remembering.

"No time for mooning, if you want your tea," said the voice above.

He went to the table, but he continued to look around, recognizing old friends. The rocking-horse with its lower lip missing. The tall wire fire-guard, and the rug in front of it. The three bars across the window. The dado procession of farmyard animals. The gas lamp purring gently above the table. A calendar showing a group of three very woolly kittens, and below, in red and black, the month—May, 1910. 1910, he reflected; that would mean he was just seven.

At the end of the meal—a somewhat dull meal, perhaps, but doubtless wholesome—Barbara asked:

"Are we going to see Mummy now?"

Nurse shook her head.

"Not now. She's out. So's your Daddy. I expect they'll look in at you when they get back—if you're good."

The whole thing was unnaturally clear and detailed: the bathing, the putting to bed. Forgotten things came back to him with an uncanny reality which be-mused him. Nurse checked her operations once to look at him searchingly and say:

"Well, you're a quiet one tonight, aren't you? I hope you're not sickening for something."

There was still no fading of the sharp impressions when he lay in bed with only the flickering night-light to show the familiar room. The dream was going on for a long time —but then dreams could do that, they could pack a whole sequence into a few seconds. Perhaps this was a special kind of dream, a sort of finale while he sat out there in the garden on that seat: it might be part of the process of dying—the kind of thing people meant when they said 'his whole life flashed before him', only it was a precious slow flash. Quite likely he had overtired himself: after all he was still only convalescent and . . .

At that moment the thought of that clerkly little man, Pendlesomething—no, Prendergast—recurred to him. It struck him with such abrupt force that he sat up in bed, looking wildly around. He pinched himself—people always did that to make sure they were awake, though he had never understood why they should not dream they were pinching themselves. It certainly felt as if he were awake. He got out of bed and stood looking about him. The floor was hard and solid under his feet, the chill in the air quite perceptible, the regular breathing of Barbara, asleep in her cot, perfectly audible. After a few moments of bewilderment he got slowly back into bed.

People who wish: "If only I had my life over again." That was what that fellow Prendergast had said . . .

Ridiculous . . . utterly absurd, of course—and, anyway, life did not begin at seven years of age—such a preposterous thing could not happen, it was against all the laws of Nature. And yet suppose . . . just suppose . . . that once, by some multi-millionth chance . . .

BOBBY Finnerson lay still, quietly contemplating an incredible vista of possibilities. He had done pretty well for himself last time merely by intelligent preception, but now, armed with foreknowledge, what might he not achieve! In on the ground floor with radio, plastics, synthetics of all kinds—with prescience of the coming wars, of the boom following the first—*and* of the 1929 slump. Aware of the trends. Knowing the weapons of the second war before it came, ready for the advent of the atomic age. Recalling endless oddments of useful information acquired haphazardly in fifty years. Where was the catch? Uneasily, he felt sure that there must be a catch: something to stop him from communicating or using his knowledge. You couldn't disorganize history, but what was it that could prevent him telling, say, the Americans about Pearl Harbor, or the French about the German plans? There must be something to stop that, but what was it?

There was a theory he had read somewhere—something about parallel universes . . .?

No. There was just one explanation for it all; in spite of seeming reality—in spite of pinching himself, it was a dream—just a dream . . . or was it?

* * *

Some hours later a board creaked outside. The quietly opened door let in a wedge of brighter light from the passage, and then shut it off. Lying still and pretending sleep, he heard careful footsteps approach. He opened his eyes to see his mother bending over him. For some moments he stared unbelievingly at her. She looked lovely in evening dress, with her eyes shining. It was with astonishment that he realized she was still barely more than a girl. She gazed down at him steadily, a little smile around her mouth. He reached up with one hand to touch her smooth cheek. Then, like a piercing bolt came the recollection of what was going to happen to her. He choked.

She leaned over and gathered him to her, speaking softly not to disturb Barbara.

"There, there, Bobby boy. There's nothing to cry about. Did I wake you suddenly? Was there a horrid dream?"

He snuffled, but said nothing.

"Never mind, darling. Dreams can't hurt you, you know. Just you forget it now, and go to sleep."

She tucked him up, kissed him lightly, and turned to the cot where Barbara lay undisturbed. A minute later she had gone.

Bobby Finnerson lay quiet but awake, gazing up at the ceiling, puzzling, and, tentatively, planning.

THE following morning, being a Saturday, involved the formality of going to the morning-room to ask for one's pocket-money. Bobby was a little shocked by the sight of his father. Not just by the absurd appearance of the tall choking collar and the high-buttoned jacket with mean lapels, but on account of his lack of distinction; he seemed a very much more ordinary young man than he had liked to remember. Uncle George was there, too, apparently as a week-end guest. He greeted Bobby heartily:

"Hullo, young man. By jingo, you've grown since I last saw you. Won't be long before you'll be helping us with the business, at this rate. How'll you like that?"

Bobby did not answer. One could not say: "That won't happen because my father's going to be killed in the war, and you are going to ruin the business through your own stupidity." So he smiled back vaguely at Uncle George, and said nothing at all.

"Do you go to school now?" his uncle added.

Bobby wondered if he did. His father came to the rescue.

"Just a kindergarten in the morning, so far," he explained.

"What do they teach you? Do you know the Kings of England?" Uncle George persisted.

"Draw it mild, George," protested Bobby's father. "Did you know 'em when you were just seven—do you now, for that matter?"

"Well, anyway, he knows who's king now, don't you, old man?" asked Uncle George.

Bobby hesitated. He had a nasty feeling that there was a trick about the question, but he had to take a chance.

"Edward the Seventh," he said, and promptly knew from their faces that it had been the wrong chance.

"I mean, George the Fifth," he amended hastily.

Uncle George nodded.

"Still sounds queer, doesn't it? I suppose they'll be putting G.R. on things soon instead of E.R."

Bobby got away from the room with his Saturday sixpence, and a feeling that it was going to be less easy than he had supposed to act his part correctly.

He had a self-protective determination not to reveal himself until he was pretty sure of his ground, particularly until he had some kind of answer to his chief perplexity:—was the knowledge he had that of the things which *must* happen, or was it of those that *ought* to happen? If it were only the former, then he would appear to be restricted to a Cassandra-like role: but if it were the latter, the possibilities were—well, was there any limit?

* * *

In the afternoon they were to play in the Square garden. They left the house by the basement door, and he helped the small Barbara with the laborious business of climbing the steps while Nurse turned back for a word with Cook. They walked across the pavement and stood waiting at the curb. The road was empty save for a high-wheeled butcher's trap bowling swiftly towards them. Bobby looked at it, and suddenly a whole horrifying scene jumped back into his memory like a vivid photograph.

He seized his little sister's arm, dragging her back towards the railings. At the same moment he saw the horse shy and begin to bolt. Barbara tripped and fell as it swerved towards them. With frightened strength he tugged her across the pavement. At the area gate he himself stumbled, but he did not let go of her arm. Somehow she fell through the gate after him, and together they rolled down the steps. A second later there was a clash of wild hooves above. A hub ripped into the railings, and slender shiny spokes flew in all directions. A single despairing yell broke from the driver as he flew out of his seat, and then the horse was away with the wreckage bumping and banging behind it, and Sunday joints littering the road.

There was a certain amount of scolding which Bobby took philosophically and forgave because Nurse and the others were all somewhat frightened. His silence covered considerable thought. They did not know, as he did, what *ought* to have happened. He knew how little Barbara *ought* to have been lying on the pavement screaming from the pain of a foot so badly mangled that it would cripple her and so poison the rest of her life. But instead she was just howling healthily from surprise and a few bumps.

That was the answer to one of his questions, and he felt a little shaky as he recognized it . . .

THEY put his ensuing 'mooniness' down to shock after the narrow escape, and did their best to rally him out of the mood.

Nevertheless, it was still on him at bedtime, for the more he looked at his situation, the more fraught with perplexity it became.

It had, amongst other things, occurred to him that he could only interfere with another person's life once. Now, for instance, by saving Barbara from that crippling injury he had entirely altered her future: there was no question of his knowledge interfering with fate's plans for her again, because he had no idea what her new future would be . . .

That caused him to reconsider the problem of his father's future. If it were to be somehow contrived that he should not be in that particular spot in France, when a shell fell there, he might not be killed at all, and if he weren't, then the question of preventing his mother from making that disastrous second marriage would never arise. Nor would Uncle George be left single-handed to ruin the business, and if the business weren't ruined the whole family circumstances would be different. They'd probably send him to a more expensive school, and thus set him on an entirely new course . . . and so on . . . and so on . . .

Bobby turned restlessly in bed. This wasn't going to be as easy as he had thought . . . it wasn't going to be at all easy . . .

If his father were to remain alive there would be a difference at every point where it touched the lives of others, widening like a series of ripples. It might not affect the big things, the pieces of solid history—but something else might. Supposing, for instance, warning were to be given of a certain assassination due to be attempted later at Sarajevo . . .?

Clearly one must keep well away from the big things. As much as possible one must flow with the previous course of events, taking advantage of them, but being careful always to disrupt them as little as possible. It would be tricky . . . very tricky indeed . . .

"Prendergast, we have a complaint. A serious complaint over XB 2832," announced the Department Director.

"I'm sorry to hear it, sir. I'm sure—"

"Not your fault. It's those Psychiatric fellows again. Get on to them, will you, and give them hell for not making a proper clearance. Tell them the fellow's dislocated one whole ganglion of lives already—and it's lucky it's only a minor ganglion. They'd better get busy, and quickly."

"Very good, sir. I'll get through at once."

Bobby Finnerson awoke, yawned, and sat up in bed. At the back of his mind there was a feeling that this was some special kind of day, like a birthday, or Christmas—only it wasn't really either of those. But it was a day when he had particularly meant to do something. If only he could remember what it was. He looked around the room and at the sunlight pouring in through the window; nothing suggested any specialness. His eyes fell on the cot where Barbara still slept peacefully. He slipped silently out of bed and across the floor. Stealthily he reached out to give a tug at the little plait which lay on the pillow.

It seemed as good as any other way of starting the day.

* * *

From time to time as he grew older that sense of specialness recurred, but he never could find any real explanation for it. In a way it seemed allied with a sensation that would come to him suddenly that he had been in a particular place before, that somehow he knew it already—even though that was not possible. As if life were a little less straightforward and obvious than it seemed. And there were similar sensations, too, flashes of familiarity over something he was doing, a sense felt sometimes, say during a conversation, that it was familiar, almost as though it had all happened before . . .

It was not a phenomenon confined to his youthful years. During both his early and later middle age it would still unexpectedly occur at times. Just a trick of the mind, they told him. Not even uncommon, they said.

"Prendergast, I see Contract XB-2832 is due for renewal again."

"Yes, sir."

"Last time, I recall, there was some little technical trouble. It might be as well to remind the Psychiatric Department in advance."

"Very good, sir."

Robert Finnerson lay dying. Two or three times before he had been under the impression that he might be dying. He had been frightened . . .

THE END

ELECTRONIC EYEBALL

SCIENCE has come up with a cheap, light, small little television camera tube called a "Vidicon" and this gadget promises to have a million new uses. Most television camera tubes at present are big, bulky, expensive things, not as sensitive to light as they might be, but the new Vidicon seems to offer almost a suitable sensitivity replacement for the human eye.

The immediate applications are obvious. Where human eyes would like to go—but can't—this tube can, in the interior of jet and rocket motors, in chemical reactions — almost anywhere.

Its cheapness makes it a possible solution to the problem of using TV in the schools as a teaching medium. Till now, the camera tube with the associated equipment was far beyond the reach of all but large organizations. The Vidicon will change that. Even ham radio stations may find a use for it.

But probably the most important immediate single use is in guided missiles. An "eye" has long been wanted. Soon the remote controlled rocket will televise back to its base all that it can see!

Illustrated by Joe W. Tillotson

TOURISTS TO TERRA

By Mack Reynolds

DIOMED of Argos, son of Tydeus, drew his sword with a shout and rushed forward to finish off his Trojan opponent before help could arrive. Suddenly he stopped and threw up a shielding arm before his eyes. When he could see again, one who could only have been Aphrodite, Goddess of love and beauty stood between him and the unconscious enemy. She was dressed as though for the bridal room, her Goddess body, breathtakingly beautiful, revealed through the transparent robe she wore. She was attired for love, but held a short sword in her hand.

Aphrodite smiled at him in derision. "Now, then, Prince of Argos, would you fight the Gods?" She advanced the sword, half mockingly.

But the Greek was mad with bloodlust, half crazed with his day's victories; he snatched up his spear, muttering, "Pallas Athene aids me," and rushed her.

They came from a far sun in a distant time, seeking thrills on alien planets. Earth was their latest stop and its puny humans promised good sport!

Her eyes widened, fear flashing in them, and she began to rise from the ground. The barbaric spear flashed out and ripped her arm; blood flowed and she dropped the sword, screaming.

Diomed heard a voice call urgently, "Go back! Go back immediately to — " And the Goddess Aphrodite disappeared.

He whirled to face the newcomer and saw another God confronting him. The extent of his action was beginning to be realized but Diomed had gone too far to turn back now; he charged his new opponent, shield held high and sword at the ready. The God lifted his hand, sending forth a bolt of power that brought the Greek to his knees.

Diomed's eyes were filled with sudden fear and despair. "Phoebus Apollo," he quavered.

The God was scornful. "Beware, Diomed," he said. "Do not think to fight with Gods."

The Greek cowered before him.

LATER, in the invisible space ship, hovering five hundred feet above the battle, Cajun faced her, his features impassive and his tone of voice faultless. He was boiling with rage beneath his courtesy.

"I will present your complaint to the Captain, but I would like to remind the Lady Jan that she has been warned repeatedly against appearing in the battle clothed as she is and without greater defenses. It was fortunate I was able to appear as soon as I did. If you'd been injured seriously, I hesitate to say what repercussions would've taken place on the home planet."

Her eyebrows went up. "Injured seriously! Just what do you mean by that? Do you realize this horrible wound will probably take half the night to heal? You saw that barbarian was insane, why didn't you come to my assistance sooner? You haven't heard the last of this, you inefficient nincompoop. When we return home I'll have you stripped of your rank!"

Cajun's face remained blank. "Yes, your ladyship," he said. "And, before I go, may I deliver a message from the Lady Marid? She said they await you in the salon."

She drew a cape about her and without speaking further, swept from the compartment.

A muscle twitched in his cheek. "Parasites," he muttered savagely, and turned to go to his own quarters where he could change from this ridiculous glittering armor, into his own uniform as ship's officer.

The Lady Jan stormed into the salon where the others had gathered to try the new concoction the steward had named ambrosia. Some of them still wore their costumes, others had changed into the more comfortable dress of their own world.

Her eyes blazed at them. "Who in the name of Makred told that Greek he would conquer anyone he fought today, even a God? The damned barbarian nearly killed me!"

The Lord Daren laughed gently. "It was Marid; she was playing the Goddess Athene. The sport was rather poor with that new bow of hers so she thought she'd inflame one of the Greeks and see just how berserk he would become if he thought he had the protection of a Goddess."

"He could have killed me!"

"Oh, come, now, Jan, you were barely scratched. Besides, Marid didn't know this Greek, Diomed, was going to run into you, or that he'd have the fantastic nerve to attack whom he thought one of his Gods."

She took up a goblet of the new drink, but she wasn't placated, "I'm of the opinion this stop shouldn't be made; it's too dangerous. I'm going to insist Captain Foren blast the city and obliterate both sides of this barbaric conflict."

THE Lady Marid, who was still dressed in her Pallas Athene armor, broke in. "Don't be so upset, Jan. We're sorry that brute hurt your arm, but what can you expect on this type of cruise? They guaranteed us thrills, didn't they? The very dangers we face are what we're paying so highly for." She laughed lightly. "Besides, that costume you wear as Aphrodite. Really! I don't know why you didn't get worse than a scratch on the arm. These Greeks aren't exactly civilized — nor exactly cold-blooded, either."

The other's face went red and she snatched another of the drinks from a tray. "Nevertheless, I'm going to complain. This war is absolutely too perilous to be part of the tour. And after all the trouble we went to in order to learn their fantastic languages and customs. Why I was under that damned Psycho-Study Impressor for nearly two hours!"

Captain Foren had entered behind her. "I agree with you Lady Jan, and can only apologize. I should've realized last week when Lord General Baris, fighting in the battle as the God Ares on the Trojan side, was speared by this same Greek. The company would never hear the end of it, if, on one of these cruises, a passenger was seriously injured."

The Lord General Baris shrugged. "It was wonderful sport. I killed a score of the beggars that day. I don't know how that one found a chink in my armor. I'll take measures against my costumer when we return home." He grinned wryly. "I doubt if the Emperor would appreciate having one of his generals killed in a primitive war, while on leave."

"I think I'll have to take a crack at this Diomed, myself," Lord Doren said.

The Lady Marid laughed. "If I know you, you'll do it with a

blaster from a hundred feet in the air above him."

Doren smiled in return. "Of course. Do you think I'd make a fool of myself by going down into their battle as Baris does? It's insane. This hand to hand conflict is much too risky."

The Captain changed the subject. "I'm sure you'll all appreciate our next stop," he said. "I plan to visit an even more astounding planet than this. We are to fight the swamp dragons of Venus."

"From what distance, Captain?" Lord Doren drawled.

The Captain smiled. "Their poisonous breath reaches half a mile, so it will be necessary to use long distance weapons."

Lord General Baris scowled. "It sounds too easy. I like to fight humanoids; there's more thrill in killing when your opponent looks like yourself, as do these earthlings."

The Lady Jan was nearing the nasty stage of intoxication. "It wouldn't be so thrilling if you weren't provided with defenses making it practically impossible to be hurt. You wouldn't enter these battles if you weren't sure you'd come out safely."

"I wouldn't deny it. Sport is sport; but I have no desire to be killed at it. At any rate, I'm opposed to killing these swamp dragons. It sounds as though it would be boring, and, Makred knows, we had enough boredom butchering those dwarfs at our last stop."

The Lady Marid backed him. She also thought Venus unattractive. If the Captain was of the opinion this war was too dangerous, wasn't there some other conflict on this planet?

The Captain told them he'd consult with his officers and let them know in the morning.

ONE thing was sure, Captain Foren thought, as he made his way toward the officer's mess. He'd have to get this group of thrill-crazy wastrels away from Troy. If one of them was hurt badly, he'd undoubtedly lose his lucrative position on the swank cruise ship.

The idea was his own, really, and a good one. In a luxury mad world the cry was for new titillations, new pleasures, new planets on which to play, new drugs to bring ever wilder dreams, new foods, new drinks, new loves; but, most of all, new thrills.

Yes, the idea of taking cruise ships of wealthy thrill seekers to the more backward planets and letting them join in primitive wars, had been his. It proved the thrill supreme. His cruises were the rage of half a dozen planets, and the company had increased his pay several times in the past few years. But he knew it could crumple like a house of cards, given one serious injury to a wealthy guest. The theory of the cruise was to let them kill without endangering themselves.

The stop at Troy, had, as a rule,

been a successful one. The Greeks and their opponents were both highly superstitious and readily accepted the presence of the aliens from space as Gods taking place in the battle. Usually, they were too terrified to take measures against the strangers in their gleaming armor, but today had been the second occasion in which a tourist had been injured, in spite of scientific, protective armor.

His officers were awaiting him in the mess hall. They too had been conscious of the wounds suffered by the thrill seeking guests, and hadn't liked it. Lady Jan was the daughter of a noble strong enough to have them all imprisoned, if the whim took him.

Captain Foren growled, "Have any of you an idea? I proposed the Venus trip, but, although they admit being leary about further risks here, they prefer fighting humanoids."

First Officer Cajun said, "Perhaps it would be better to head for the home planet, Captain."

Captain Foren shook his head. "We can't do that; the cruise has another week to go. If we went back now it would be obvious that something had happened and just bring matters to a head. If we can give them another week of thrills, possibly they'll have forgotten their wounds by the time we return."

The Chief Engineer turned to Cajun. "At what stage of development is this planet?"

"I believe it's at H-2. Why?"

"I was wondering at the possibility of going forward a few thousand years in time and participating in a war that dealt less in hand to hand conflict. They could have their fill of killing, with a minimum of danger—protected, of course, with suitable anti-projectile force fields."

CAJUN went over to the ship's Predictinformer and spoke into its mouthpiece. "What will be the military development of this planet in two or three thousand years; and would it be safe to take the ship into that period?"

They awaited the answer, which came approximately one minute later. "Probability shows the inhabitants of Terra will begin utilizing explosives for propelling missiles in two thousand years. About five hundred years later they will have developed this means of warfare to its ultimate. Safety for the ship is indicated."

Captain Foren mused, "That sounds practical. We could participate in some war in which our passengers could use such weapons as snipers, from a distance." Another thought struck him. "Besides, the Lord General Baris is quite intrigued with the possibilities involved in fighting the humanoids here. He had spoken of transporting large numbers of his troops to Terra and using the planet for a training ground in actual combat. Undoubtedly, the earthlings of the future would make better victims for his soldiers than these more primitive types. It might be well to look at the future of this planet."

The First Engineer said, "Such a step would wipe out the development of civilization on the planet."

Captain Foren shrugged impatiently. He ordered Cajun to make immediate preparations to take the ship forward twenty-five hundred years, and gave instructions to a sub-officer to locate a suitable conflict as soon as they arrived, so that the guests could begin their participation when they awoke in the morning.

The ship arrived effortlessly in its new location in time, but when the sub-officer returned from his patrol, First Officer Cajun took him to the Captain's quarters himself.

He saluted. "I don't believe this is quite it, Captain."

"Why not? Weren't there any wars in progress?"

Cajun said, "It wasn't that. There were several. They don't seem to have reached the development for which we were looking. For instance, in the region in which we've landed, the first stage of a conflict between two nations have begun. The countries are called Mexico and the United States and they're fighting over the northwestern possessions of the former, although, as always, both sides claim they are involved for idealistic reasons. However, the fighting still consists, to an extent, of hand to hand conflict. The soldiers carry explosive propelled missile weapons, but they're usually slow in loading and single shot in operation. Swords are carried at the ends of these weapons so that after it is fired the soldier may dash forward and engage his enemy personally."

The Captain was glum. "That's as bad as before, and I can't risk our passengers in any more hand to hand combat."

"Sir, these humanoids on Terra seem slow in progressing but I have an idea if we move forward another hundred years they will be using automatic weapons, and hand to hand combat will be antiquated. The calendar system they use calls this the year 1845. I suggest we travel forward to 1945.

Captain Foren made a snap decision. "All right, we'll go forward a century. As soon as we arrive, have a patrol go out again."

WHEN Captain Foren awoke in the morning, the hot desert sun was already well into the sky. The invisible space ship had stationed itself a hundred feet off the ground in an area in which there were no signs of habitation and few of the works of man. He strode leisurely to the control room and returned the greetings of the morning watch.

"Any word from the patrol as yet?" he asked.

First Officer Cajun was worried. "No, sir, and he should've been back long before this."

"I trust nothing has happened to him. Has he reported at all?"

"Only once, several hours ago. Evidently there is a globewide war raging." Cajun ran his tongue over thin lips. "Our passengers should have excellent sport. In fact, Captain, if you can spare me, I would like to participate myself."

Captain Foren looked at him and laughed. "You, also? I'm afraid this must be a racial characteristic, this love of imposing death. I must confess, on my first trips, I too liked to join in the sport." He turned and glanced out an observation port. "What is that steel tower down there on the desert?"

"We couldn't decide, Captain, unless it's some structure for conducting tests of some sort or other. The surprising thing about it is that our instruments detect radioactivity . . . "

The Captain interrupted sharply, "Has anyone checked the ship's Predictinformer on whether or not this era is completely safe?"

Cajun said, "I assumed that you had, sir." He stepped to the instrument and spoke into its mouthpiece. "What is the military development of this planet? Is the ship safe?"

The Predictinformer began its report. "In the past thirty-five years military science on Terra has developed tremendously under the impetus of two world-wide conflicts. At present the dominant power on this continent is experimenting with nuclear fission . . . '"

Sudden fear came into the eyes of the captain of the thrill ship. "That radioactive steel tower! Blast off," he shrieked, "Blast off!"

The Predictinformer went on dispassionately, " . . . and is about to test an atomic bomb against which this ship's defenses would be . . . "

It got no further.

THE END

"WHAT SO PROUDLY WE HAIL..."

By DAY KEENE

The Pig and Whistle of 1789 was a far cry from Central Park in 1950. And Ephraim Hale was certain that more than rum had been used to get him there!

EPHRAIM Hale yawned a great yawn and awakened. He'd expected to have a head. Surprisingly, considering the amount of hot buttered rum he'd consumed the night before, he had none. But where in the name of the Continental Congress had he gotten to this time? The last he remembered was parting from Mr. Henry in front of the Pig and Whistle. A brilliant statesman, Mr. Henry.

"Give me liberty or give me death."

Illustrated by H. W. McCauley

He stared at the girl in amazement, for he had never seen such brazen nakedness in all his life—and such real beauty . . .

E-yah. But that didn't tell him where he was. It looked like a cave. This sort of thing had to stop. Now he was out of the Army and in politics he had to be more circumspect. Ephraim felt in his purse, felt flesh, and every inch of his six feet two blushed crimson. This, Martha would never believe.

He sat up on the floor of the cave. The thief who had taken his clothes had also stolen his purse. He was naked and penniless. And he the representative from Middlesex to the first Congress to convene in New York City in this year of our Lord, 1789.

He searched the floor of the cave. All the thief had left, along with his home-cobbled brogans, his Spanish pistol, and the remnants of an old leather jerkin, was the post from Sam Osgood thanking him for his support in helping to secure Osgood's appointment as Postmaster General.

Forming a loin cloth of the leather, Ephraim tucked the pistol and cover in it. The letter could prove valuable. A man in politics never knew when a friend might need reminding. Then, decent as possible under the circumstances, he walked toward the distant point of light to reconnoiter his position. It was bad. His rum-winged feet had guided him into a gentleman's park. And the gentleman was prolific. A dozen boys of assorted ages were playing at ball on the greensward.

Rolling aside the rock that formed a natural door to the cave, Ephraim beckoned the nearest boy, a cherub of about seven. "I wonder, young master, if you would tell me on whose estate I am trespassing."

The boy grinned through a maze of freckles. "Holy smoke, mister. What you out front for? A second Nature Boy, or Tarzan Comes To Television?"

"I beg your pardon?" Ephraim said puzzled.

"Ya heard me," the boy said.

CLOSE up, he didn't look so cherubic. He was one of the modern generation with no respect for his elders. What he needed was a beech switch well applied to the seat of his britches. Ephraim summoned the dignity possible to a man without pants. "I," he attempted to impress the boy, "am the Honorable Ephraim Hale, late officer of the Army of The United States, and elected representative from Middlesex to Congress. And I will be beholden to you, young sir, if you will inform your paternal parent a gentleman is in distress and wouldst have words with him."

"Aw, ya fadder's mustache," the boy said. "Take it to the V.A. I should lose the old man a day of hackin'." So saying, he returned to cover second base.

Ephraim was tempted to pursue and cane him. He might if it hadn't been for the girl. While he had been talking to the boy she had strolled across the greensward to a sunny knoll not far from the mouth of the cave. She was both young and comely. As he watched, fascinated, she began to disrobe. The top part of her dress came off revealing a bandeau of like material barely covering her firm young breasts. Then, stepping out of her skirt, she stood a moment in bandeau and short flared pants, her arms stretched in obeisance to the sun before reclining on the grass.

Ephraim blushed furiously. He hadn't seen as much of Martha during their ten years of marriage. He cleared his throat to make his presence known and permit her to cover her charms.

The girl turned her head toward him. "Hello. You taking a sun bath, too? It's nice to have it warm so oily, ain't it?"

Ephraim continued to blush. The girl continued to look, and liked what she saw. With a pair of pants and a whiskey glass the big man in the mouth of the cave could pass as a man of distinction. If his hair was long, his forehead was high and his cheeks were gaunt and clean shaven. His shoulders were broad and well-muscled and his torso tapered to a V. It wasn't every day a girl met so handsome a man. She smiled. "My name's Gertie Swartz. What's yours?"

Swallowing the lump in his throat, Ephraim told her.

"That's a nice name," she approved. "I knew a family named Hale in Greenpernt. But they moved up to Riverside Height. Ya live in the Heights?"

Ephraim tried to keep from looking at her legs. "No. I reside on a farm, a league or so from Perth Amboy."

"Oh. Over in Joisey, huh?" Gertie was mildly curious. "Then what ya doin' in New York in that Johnny Weismuller outfit?"

"I," Ephraim sighed, "was robbed."

The girl sat up, clucking sympathetically. "Imagine. Right in Central Park. Like I was saying to Sadie just the other night, there ought to be a law. A mugger cleaned you, huh?"

A bit puzzled by her reference to a *crocodilus palustris,* but emboldened by her friendliness, Ephraim came out of the cave and sat on the paper beside her. Her patois was strange but not unpleasant. Swartz was a German name. The blond girl was probably the offspring of some Hessian. Even so she was a pretty little doxy and he hadn't bussed a wench for some time. He slipped an experimental arm around her waist. "Haven't we met before?"

GERTIE removed his arm and slapped him without heat. "No. And no hard feelings, understand. Ya can't blame a guy for trying." She saw the puckered white scars on his chest, souvenirs of King's Mountain. "Ya was in the Army, huh?"

"Five years."

She was amazed and pleased. "Now ain't that a coincidence? Ya probably know my brother Benny. He was in five years, too." Gertie was concerned. "You were drinking last night, huh?"

"To my shame."

Gertie made the soft clucking sound again. "How ya going to get home in that outfit?"

"That," Ephraim said, "is the problem."

She reached for and put on her skirt. "Look. I live just over on 82nd. And if ya want, on account of you both being veterans, I'll lend you one of Benny's suits." She wriggled into the top part of her four piece sun ensemble. "Benny's about the same size as you. Wait."

Smiling, Ephraim watched her go across the greensward to a broad turnpike bisecting the estate, then rose in sudden horror as a metallic-looking monster with sightless round glass eyes swooped out from behind a screen of bushes and attempted to run her down. The girl dodged it adroitly, paused in the middle of the pike to allow a stream of billings-gate to escape her sweet red lips, then continued blithely on her way.

His senses alerted, Ephraim continued to watch the pike. The monsters were numerous as locusts and seemed to come in assorted colors and sizes. Then he spotted a human in each and realized what they must be. While he had lain in a drunken stupor, Mother Shipton's prophecy had come true——

'Carriages without horses shall go.'

He felt sick. The malcontents would, undoubtedly, try to blame *this* on the administration. He had missed the turning of an important page of history. He lifted his eyes above the budding trees and was almost sorry he had. The trees alone were familiar. A solid rectangle of buildings hemmed in what he had believed to be an estate; unbelievable buildings. Back of them still taller buildings lifted their spires and Gothic towers and one stubby thumb into the clouds. His pulse quickening, he looked at the date line of a paper on the grass. It was April 15, 1950.

He would never clank cups with Mr. Henry again. The fiery Virginian, along with his cousin Nathan, and a host of other good and true men, had long since become legends. He should be dust. It hadn't been a night since he had parted from Mr. Henry. It had been one hundred and sixty-one years.

A wave of sadness swept him. The warm wind off the river seemed cooler. The sun lost some of its warmth. He had never felt so alone. Then he forced himself to face it. How many times had he exclaimed:

"If only I could come back one hundred years from now."

Well, here he was, with sixty-one years for good measure.

A white object bounded across the grass toward him. Instinctively Ephraim caught it and found it was the hard white sphere being used by the boys playing at ball.

"All the way," one of them yelled.

Ephraim cocked his arm and threw. The sphere sped like a rifle ball toward the target of the most distant glove, some seventeen rods away.

"Wow!" the youth to whom he had spoken admired. The young voice was so shocked with awe Ephraim had an uneasy feeling the boy was about to genuflect. "Gee. Get a load of that whip. The guy's got an arm like Joe DiMaggio . . . "

SUPPER was good but over before Ephraim had barely got started. Either the American stomach had shrunk or Gertie and her brother, despite their seeming affluence, were among the very poor. There had only been two vegetables, one meat, no fowl or venison, no hoe cakes, no mead or small ale or rum, and only one pie and one cake for the three of them.

He sat, still hungry, in the parlor thinking of Martha's ample board and generous bed, realizing she, too, must be dust. There was no use in returning to Middlesex. It would be as strange and terrifying as New York.

Benny offered him a small paper spill of tobacco. "Sis tells me ya was in the Army. What outfit was ya with?" Before Ephraim could tell him, he continued, "Me, I was one of the bastards of Bastonge." He dug a thumb into Ephraim's ribs. "Pretty hot, huh, what Tony McAuliffe tells the Krauts when they think they got us where the hair is short and want we should surrender."

"What did he tell them?" Ephraim asked politely.

Benny looked at him suspiciously. " 'Nuts!' he tol' 'em. 'Nuts.' Ya sure ya was in the Army, chum?"

Ephraim said he was certain.

"E.T.O. or Pacific?"

"Around here," Ephraim said. "You know, Germantown, Monmouth, King's Mountain."

"Oh. State's side, huh?" Benny promptly lost all interest in his sister's guest. Putting his hat on the back of his head he announced his bloody intention of going down to the corner and shooting one of the smaller Kelly Pools.

"Have a good time," Gertie told him.

Sitting down beside Ephraim she fiddled with the knobs on an ornate commode and a diminuative muleskinner appeared out of nowhere cracking a bull whip and shouting something almost unintelligible about having a Bible in his pack for the Reverend Mr. Black.

Ephraim shied away from the commode, wide-eyed.

Gertie fiddled with the knobs again and the little man went away. "Ya don't like television, huh?"

She moved a little closer to him. "Ya want we should just sit and talk?"

Patting at the perspiration on his forehead with one of Benny's handkerchiefs, Ephraim said, "That would be fine."

As with the horseless carriages, the towering buildings, and the water that ran out of taps hot or cold as you desired, there was some logical explanation for the little man. But he had swallowed all the wonders he was capable of assimilating in one night.

Gertie moved still closer. "Wadda ya wanna talk about?"

Ephraim considered the question. He wanted to know if the boys had ever been able to fund or reduce the national debt. Seventy-four million, five hundred and fifty-five thousand, six hundred and forty-one dollars was a lot of money. He wanted to know if Mr. Henry had been successful in his advocation of the ten amendments to the Constitution, here-in-after to be known as the Bill Of Rights, and how many states had ratified them. He wanted to know the tax situation and how the public had reacted to the proposed imposition of a twenty-five cent a gallon excise tax on whiskey.

"What," he asked Gertie, "would you say was the most important thing that happened this past year?"

Gertie considered the question. "Well, Rita Hayworth had a baby and Clark Gable got married."

"I mean politically."

"Oh. Mayor O'Dwyer got married."

Gertie had been very kind. Gertie was very lovely. Ephraim meant to see more of her. With Martha fluttering around in heaven exchanging receipts for chow chow and watermelon preserves, there was no reason why he shouldn't. But as with modern wonders, he'd had all of Gertie he could take for one night. He wanted to get out into the city and find out just what had happened during the past one hundred and sixty-one years.

Gertie was sorry to see him go. "But ya will be back, won't you, Ephraim?"

He sealed the promise with a kiss. "Tomorrow night. And a good many nights after that." He made hay on what he had seen the sun shine. "You're very lovely, my dear."

She slipped a bill into the pocket of his coat. "For the Ferry-fare back to Joisey." There were lighted candles in her eyes. "Until tomorrow night, Ephraim."

THE streets were even more terrifying than they had been in the daytime. Ephraim walked east on 82nd Street, south on Central Park West, then east on Central Park South. He'd had it in mind to locate the Pig and Whistle. Realizing the futility of such an attempt he stopped in at the next place he came to exuding a familiar aroma and laying the dollar Gertie had slipped into his pocket on the bar, he ordered, "Rum."

The first thing he had to do was find gainful employment. As a Harvard graduate, lawyer, and former Congressman, it shouldn't prove too difficult. He might, in time, even run for office again. A congressman's six dollars per diem wasn't to be held lightly.

A friendly, white-jacketed, Mine Host set his drink in front of him and picked up the bill. "I thank you, sir."

About to engage him in conversation concerning the state of the nation, Ephraim looked from Mine Host to the drink, then back at Mine Host again. "E-yah. I should think you would thank me. I'll have my change if you please. Also a man-sized drink."

No longer so friendly, Mine Host leaned across the wood. "That's an ounce and a half. What change? Where did you come from Reuben? What did you expect to pay?"

"The usual price. A few pennies a mug," Ephraim said. "The war is over. Remember? And with the best imported island rum selling wholesale at twenty cents a gallon——"

Mine Host picked up the shot glass and returned the bill to the bar. "You win. You've had enough, pal. What do you want to do, cost me my license? Go ahead. Like a good fellow. Scram."

He emphasized the advice by putting the palm of his hand in Ephraim's face, pushing him toward the door. It was a mistake. Reaching across the bar, Ephraim snaked Mine Host out from behind it and was starting to shake some civility into the publican when he felt a heavy hand on his shoulder.

"Let's let it go at that, chum."

"Drunk and disorderly, eh?" a second voice added.

The newcomers were big men, men who carried themselves with the unmistakable air of authority. He attempted to explain and one of them held his arms while the other man searched him and found the Spanish pistol.

"Oh. Carrying a heater, eh? That happens to be against the law, chum."

"Ha," Ephraim laughed at him. "Also ho." He quoted from memory Article II of the amendments Mr. Henry had read him in the Pig and Whistle:

"'A well-regulated militia being necessary to the security of a free state the right of the people to keep and bear Arms shall not be infringed'."

"Now he's a militia," the plainclothes man said.

"He's a nut," his partner added.

"Get him out of here," Mine Host said.

EPHRAIM sat on the bunk in his cell, deflated. This was a fine resurrection for a member of the First Congress.

"Cheer up," a voice from the upper bunk consoled. "The worst they can do is burn you." He offered Ephraim a paper spill of tobacco. "The name is Silovitz."

Ephraim asked him why he was in gaol.

"Alimony," the other man sighed. "That is the non-payment thereof."

The word was new to Ephraim. He asked Silovitz to explain. "But that's illegal, archaic. You can't be jailed for debt."

His cell mate lighted a cigarette. "No. Of course not. Right now I'm sitting in the Stork Club buying Linda Darnell a drink." He studied Ephraim's face. "Say, I've been wondering who you look like. I make you now. You look like the statue of Nathan Hale the D.A.R. erected in Central Park."

"It's a family resemblance," Ephraim said. "Nat was a second cousin. They hung him in '76, the same year I went into the Army."

Silovitz nodded approval. "That's a good yarn. Stick to it. The wife of the judge you'll probably draw is an ardent D.A.R. But if I were you I'd move my war record up a bit and remove a few more cousins between myself and Nathan."

He smoked in silence a minute. "Boy. It must have been nice to live back in those days. A good meal for a dime. Whiskey, five cents a drink. No sales or income or surtax. No corporate or excise profits tax. No unions, no John L., no check-off. No tax on diapers and coffins. No closed shops. No subsidies. No paying farmers for cotton they didn't plant or for the too many potatoes they did. No forty-two billion dollar budget."

"I beg your pardon?" Ephraim said.

"Ya heard me." Swept by a nostalgia for something he'd never known, Silovitz continued. "No two hundred and sixty-five billion national debt. No trying to spend ourselves out of the poor house. No hunting or fishing or driving or occupational license. No supporting three-fourths of Europe and Asia. No atom bomb. No Molotov. No Joe Stalin. No alimony. No Frankie Sinatra. No video. No bebop."

His eyes shone. "No New Dealers, Fair Dealers, Democrats, Jeffersonian Democrats, Republicans, State's Righters, Communists, Socialists, Socialist - Labor, Farmer - Labor, American - Labor, Liberals, Progressives and Prohibitionists and W.C.T.U.ers. Congress united and fighting to make this a nation." He quoted the elderly gentleman from Pennsylvania. "'We must all hang together, or assuredly we shall all hang separately.' Ah. Those were the days."

Ephraim cracked his knuckles. It was a pretty picture but, according to his recollection, not exactly correct. The boys had hung together pretty well during the first few weeks after the signing of the Declaration Of Independence. But from there on in it had been a dog fight. No two delegates had been able to agree on even the basic articles of confederation. The Constitution itself was a patch work affair and compromise drafted originally as a preamble and seven Articles by delegates from twelve of the thirteen states at the May '87 convention in Philadelphia. And as for the boys hanging together, the first Congress had convened on March 4th and it had been April 6th before a quorum had been present.

Silovitz sighed. "Still, it's the little things that get ya. If only Bessie hadn't insisted on listening to 'When A Girl Marries' when I wanted to hear the B-Bar-B Riders. And if only I hadn't made that one bad mistake."

"What was that?" Ephraim asked.

Silovitz told him. "I snuck up to the Catskills to hide out on the court order. And what happens? A game warden picks me up because I forgot to buy a two dollar fishing license!"

A free man again. Ephraim stood on the walk in front of the 52nd Street Station diverting outraged pedestrians into two rushing streams as he considered his situation. It hadn't been much of a trial. The arresting officers admitted the pistol was foul with rust and probably hadn't been fired since O'Sullivan was a gleam in his great-great grandfather's eyes.

"Ya name is Hale. An' ya a veteran, uh?" the judge had asked.

"Yes," Ephraim admitted, "I am." He'd followed Silovitz's advice. "What's more, Nathan Hale was a relation of mine."

The judge had beamed. "Ya don' say. Ya a Son Of The Revolution, uh?"

On Ephraim admitting he was and agreeing with the judge the ladies of the D.A.R. had the right to stop someone named Marion Anderson from singing in Constitution Hall if they wanted to, the judge, running for re-election, had told him to go and drink no more, or if he had to drink not to beef about his bill.

"Ya got ya state bonus and ya N.S.L.I. refund didncha?"

Physically and mentally buffeted by his night in a cell and Silovitz's revelation concerning the state of the nation, Ephraim stood frightened by the present and aghast at the prospect of the future.

Only two features of his resurrection pleased him. Both were connected with Gertie. Women, thank God, hadn't changed. Gertie was very lovely. With Gertie sharing his board and bed he might manage to acclimate himself and be about the business of every good citizen, begetting future toilers to pay off the national debt. It wasn't an unpleasing prospect. He had, after all, been celibate one hundred and sixty-one years. Still, with rum at five dollars a fifth, eggs eighty cents a dozen, and lamb chops ninety-five cents a pound, marriage would run into money. He had none. Then he thought of Sam Osgood's letter . . .

MR. Le Duc Neimors was so excited he could hardly balance his pince-nez on the aquiline bridge of his well-bred nose. It was the first time in the multi-millionaire's experience as a collector of Early Americana he had ever heard of, let alone been offered, a letter purported to have been written by the First Postmaster General, franked by the First Congress, and containing a crabbed foot-note by the distinguished patriot from Pennsylvania who was credited with being the founding father of the postal system. He read the foot-note aloud:

Friend Hale:

May I add my gratitude to Sam's for your help in this matter. I have tried to convince him it is almost certain to degenerate into a purely political office as a party whip and will bring him as many headaches as it will dollars or honors. However, as 'Poor Richard' says, 'Experience keeps a dear school, but fools will learn in no other'.

Cordially,

Ben

The multi-millionaire was frank. "If this letter and cover are genuine, they have, from the collector's viewpoint, almost incalculable historic and philatelic value." He showed the sound business sense that, along with marrying a wealthy widow and two world wars, he had been able to pyramid a few loaves of bread and seven pounds of hamburger into a restaurant and chain-grocery empire. "But I won't pay a penny more than, say, two hundred and twenty-five thousand dollars. And that only after an expert of my choice has authenticated both the letter and the cover."

Weinfield, the dealer to whom Ephraim had gone, swallowed hard. "That will be satisfactory."

"E-yah," Ephraim agreed.

He went directly to 82nd Street to press his suit with Gertie. It wasn't a difficult courtship. Gertie was tired of reading the Kinsey Report and eager to learn more about life at first hand. The bastard of Bastogne was less enthusiastic. If another male was to be added to the family he would have preferred one from the Eagle or 10th Armored Division or the 705th Tank Destroyer Battalion. However on learning his prospective brother-in-law was about to come into a quarter of a million dollars, minus Weinfield's commission, he thawed to the extent of loaning Ephraim a thousand dollars, three hundred and seventy-five of which Gertie insisted Ephraim pay down on a second-hand car.

IT was a busy but happy week. There was the matter of learning to drive. There were blood tests to take. There was an apartment to find. Ephraim bought a marriage license, a car license, a driver's license, and a dog license for the blond cocker spaniel that Gertie saw and admired. The principle of easy credit explained to him, he paid twenty-five dollars down and agreed to pay five dollars a week for four years, plus a nominal carrying charge, for a one thousand five hundred dollar diamond engagement ring. He paid ten dollars more on a three-piece living room suite and fifteen dollars down on a four hundred and fifty dollar genuine waterfall seven-piece bedroom outfit. Also, at Gertie's insistence, he pressed a one hundred dollar bill into a rental agent's perspiring palm to secure a two room apartment because it was still under something Gertie called rent control.

His feet solidly on the ground of the brave new America in which he had awakened, Ephraim, for the life of him, couldn't see what Silovitz had been beefing about. E-yah. Neither a man nor a nation could stay stationary. Both had to move with the times. They'd had Silovitz's at Valley Forge, always yearning for the good old days. Remembering their conversation, however, and having reserved the bridal suite at a swank Catskill resort, Ephraim, purely as a precautionary measure, along with his other permits and licenses, purchased a fishing license to make certain nothing would deter or delay the inception of the new family he intended to found.

The sale of Sam Osgood's letter was consummated the following Monday at ten o'clock in Mr. Le Duc Neimors' office. Ephraim and Gertie were married at nine in the City Hall and after a quick breakfast of dry martinis she waited in the car with Mr. Gorgeous while Ephraim went up to get the money. The multi-millionaire had it waiting, in cash.

"And there you are. Two hundred and twenty-five thousand dollars."

Ephraim reached for the stacked sheaves of bills, wishing he'd brought a sack, and a thin-faced man with a jaundice eye introduced himself. "Jim Carlyle is the name." He showed his credentials. "Of the Internal Revenue Bureau. And to save any possible complication, I'll take Uncle Sam's share right now." He sorted the sheaves of bills into piles. "We want $156,820 plus $25,000, or a total of $179,570, leaving a balance of $45,430."

Ephraim looked at the residue sourly and a jovial man slapped his back and handed him a card. "New York State Income Tax, Mr. Hale. But we won't be hogs. We'll let you off easy. All we want is 2% up to the first $1,000, 3% on the next $2,000, 4% on the next $2,000,

5% on the next $2,000, 6% on the next $2,000, and 7% on everything over $9,000. If my figures are correct, and they are, I'll take $2,930.10." He took it. Then, slapping Ephraim's back again, he laughed. "Leaving, $42,499.90."

"Ha ha," Ephraim laughed weakly.

MR. Weinfield dry-washed his hands. "Now we agreed on a 15% commission. That is, 15% of the whole. And 15% of $225,000 is $32,750 you owe me."

"Take it," Ephraim said. Mr. Weinfield did and Ephraim wished he hadn't eaten the olive in his second martini. It felt like it had gone to seed and was putting out branches in his stomach. In less than five minutes his quarter of a million dollars had shrunk to $9,749.90. By the time he paid for the things he had purchased and returned Benny's $1,000 he would be back where he'd started.

Closing his case, Mr. Carlyle asked, "By the way, Mr. Hale. Just for the record. Where did you file your report last year?"

"I didn't," Ephraim admitted. "This is the first time I ever paid income tax."

Mr. Le Duc Neimors looked shocked. The New York State man looked shocked. Mr. Weinfield looked shocked.

"Oh," Carlyle said. "I see. Well in that case I'd better take charge of this too." He added the sheaves remaining on the desk to those already in his case and fixed Ephraim with his jaundiced eye. "We'll expect you down at the bureau as soon as it's convenient, Mr. Hale. If there was no deliberate intent on your part to defraud, it may be that your lawyers still can straighten this out without us having to resort to criminal prosecution."

Gertie was stroking the honey-colored Mr. Gorgeous when Ephriam got back to the car. "Ya got it, honey?"

"Yeah," Ephriam said shortly. "I got it."

He jerked the car away from the curb so fast he almost tore out the aged rear end. Her feelings hurt, Gertie sniveled audibly until they'd crossed the George Washington Bridge. Then, having suffered in comparative silence as long as she could, she said, "Ya didn't need to bite my head off, Ephraim. And on our honeymoon, too. All I done was ast ya a question."

"Did," Ephraim corrected her.

"Did what?" Gertie asked.

Ephraim turned his head to explain the difference between the past tense and the participle "have done" and Gertie screamed as he almost collided head on with a car going the other way. Mr. Gorgeous yelped and bit Ephraim on the arm. Then, both cars and excitement being new to the twelve week old puppy, he was most inconveniently sick.

On their way again, Ephraim

apologized. "I'm sorry I was cross." He was. None of this was Gertie's fault. She couldn't help it if he'd been a fool. There was no need of spoiling her honeymoon. The few hundred in his pockets would cover their immediate needs. And he'd work this out somehow. Things had looked black at Valley Forge, too.

Gertie snuggled closer to him. "Ya do love me, don't ya?"

"Devotedly," Ephraim assured her. He tried to put his arm around her. Still suspicious, Mr. Gorgeous bit him again. Mr. Gorgeous, Eprraim could see, was going to be a problem.

His mind continued to probe the situation as he drove. Things had come to a pretty pass when a nation this size was insolvent, when out-go and deficit spending so far exceeded current revenue, taxes had become confiscatory. There was mismanagement somewhere. There were too many feet under the table. Too many were eating too high off the hog. Perhaps what Congress needed was some of the spirit of '76 and '89. A possible solution of his own need for a job occurred to him. "How," he asked Gertie, "would you like to be the wife of a Congressman?"

"I think we have a flat tire," she answered. "Either that, honey, or one of the wheels isn't quite round on the bottom."

SHE walked Mr. Gorgeous while he changed the tire. It was drizzling by the time they got back in the car. Both the cowl and the top leaked. A few miles past Bear Mountain, it rained. It was like riding in a portable needle-shower. All human habitation blotted out by the rain, the rugged landscape was familiar to Ephraim. He'd camped under that great oak when it had been a young tree. He'd fought on the crest of that hill over-looking the river. But what in the name of time had he been fighting for?

He felt a new wave of tenderness for Gertie. This was the only world the child had ever known. A world of video and installment payments, of automobiles and war, of atom bombs and double-talk and meaningless jumbles of figures. A world of confused little men and puzzled, barren, women.

"I love you, Gertie," he told her.

She wiped the rain out of her eyes and smiled at him. "I love you, too. And it's all right with me to go on. But I think we'd better stop pretty soon. I heard Mr. Gorgeous sneeze and I'm afraid he's catching cold."

Damn Mr. Gorgeous, Ephraim thought. Still, there was sense in what she said. The rain was blinding. He could barely see the road. And somewhere he'd made a wrong turning. They'd have to stop where they could.

The hotel was small and old and might once have been an Inn. Ephraim got Gertie inside, signed the yellowed ledger, and saw her and

Mr. Gorgeous installed in a room with a huge four poster bed before going back for the rest of the luggage.

A dried-up descendant of Cotton Mather, the tobacco chewing proprietor was waiting at the foot of the stairs when he returned sodden with rain and his arms and hands filled with bags.

"Naow, don't misunderstand me, Mr. Hale," the old witch-burner said, "I don't like t' poke m' nose intuh other people's business. But I run a respectable hotel an I don't cater none t' fly-b'-nights or loose women." He adjusted the glasses on his nose. "Y' sure y' an' Mrs. Hale are married? Y' got anythin' t' prove it?"

Ephraim counted to ten. Then still half-blinded by the rain dripping from the brim of his Homburg he set the bags on the floor, took an envelope from his pocket, selected a crisp official paper, gave it to the hotel man, picked up the bags again and climbed the stairs to Gertie.

She'd taken off her wet dress and put on a sheer negligee that set Ephraim's pulse to pounding. He took off his hat, eased out of his sodden coat and tossed it on a chair.

"Did I ever tell you I loved you?"

Gertie ran her fingers through his hair. "Go ahead. Tell me again."

Tilting her chin, Ephraim kissed her. This was good. This was right. This was all that mattered. He'd make Gertie a good husband. He—

A furtive rap on the door sidetracked his train of thought. He opened it to find the old man in the hall, shaking as with palsy. "Now a look a yere, Mister," he whispered. "If y' ain't done it, don't do it. Jist pack yer bags and git." One palsied hand held out the crisp piece of paper Ephraim had given him. "This yere fishin' license ain't for it."

Ephraim looked from the fishing license to his coat. The envelope had fallen on the floor, scattering its contents. A foot away, under the edge of the bed, his puppy eyes sad, Mr. Gorgeous was thoughtfully masticating the last of what once had been another crisp piece of paper. As Ephraim watched, Mr. Gorgeous burped, and swallowed. It was, as Silovitz had said, the little things.

IT was three nights later, at dusk, when Mickey spotted the apparition. For a moment he was startled. Then he knew it for what it was. It was Nature Boy, back in costume, clutching a jug of rum to his bosom.

"Hey, Mister," Mickey stopped Ephraim. "I been looking all over for you. My cousin's a scout for the Yankees. And when I told him about your whip he said for you to come down to the stadium and show 'em what you got."

Ephraim looked at the boy glass-eyed.

Mickey was hurt by his lack of enthusiasm. "Gee. Ain't you excited? Wouldn't you like to be a big league ball player, the idol of every red-blooded American boy? Wouldn't you like to make a lot of money and have the girls crazy about you?"

The words reached through Ephraim's fog and touched a responsive chord. Drawing himself up to his full height he clutched the jug still tighter to his bosom with all of the dignity possible to a man without pants.

"Ya fadder's mustache," he said.

Then staggering swiftly into the cave he closed the rock door firmly and finally behind him.

THE END

MIDGET MARVELS

WE'VE often reported on the amazing revolution taking place in the field of electronics with the introduction of the transistor. You may remember this ingenious little gadget as nothing more than a piece of the element germanium touched by three tungsten wires which behaves exactly like a three electrode vacuum tube in a radio or a television set! Put small voltages in one end of this thing, and they come out bigger at the other end. This miracle of applied science is contributing directly to everyone's benefit by making scientific gadetry more reliable and tremendously smaller.

And because no heating element is needed, apparatus runs cooler and more efficiently. Well, the end isn't yet in sight. Along comes the announcement that the transistor effect has been applied to the photoelectric cell!

Here a piece of germanium is touched by a single wire and light allowed to shine on the other side of the crystal. Vary the intensity of the light and the electric voltage across the germanium phototransistor varies.

Cheap, rugged, compact, the phototransistor along with the transistor itself makes an irresistible combination for any sort of an electronic device.

Because so many robotic, remote controlled devices are coming into use, tough simple gadgets are necessary. Technology is producing them. Apparently the field is only beginning to be scratched too.

If you want a concrete picture of what the future is going to be like, you don't have to strain your mind. We've got many of the things here already. Radio and TV along with all the other gadgetry will be vastly improved, but the main thing to remember is that the size of everything will cut to a small fraction of its present bulk. The biggest most complex computing machines, business machines, electronic devices and so on, will be reduced in size by factors of one or two or even ten. You'll carry around a complete powerful transmitter receiver in a matchbox, while a TV set will occupy no more space than a miniature table model radio.

The only thing that is likely to grow much bigger in the future is the size of swelled heads!

Illustrated by Bill Terry

THE ULTIMATE QUEST

By Hal Annas

Man has evolved slowly, always striving toward a nebulous goal somewhere in his future. Will he attain it — to regret it? . . .

STRIDING down the corridor on long thin legs, Art Fillmore mentally glanced over the news and his wide brow puckered. "Scientists to awaken twentieth century man," the mental beam proclaimed. "Dark age to yield untold volumes of ignorance."

Fillmore paused before the twelve-foot door, closed his eyes and concentrated until he had achieved the proper attenuation, then entered the office without opening the door. The bald man in the reclining chair dropped his feet from the five-foot-high desk and sat up with a start.

"I wish you wouldn't do that, Art," he said nervously. "You know I've got the itch."

"Sorry," Fillmore apologized. "Wasn't thinking. Had my mind on my forthcoming wedding."

"Wedding?" The bald man's narrow mouth dropped open, revealing small fragile teeth. "Why didn't you tell me? What does she look like?"

"Haven't seen her yet," Fillmore

grinned. "Just mental images, and you know how girls are when they project their own images. But she's a mental pippin: seven feet eight or nine with a shape you dream about. Must weigh about eighty-two or three pounds."

"Too fat," the bald man grunted. "I never liked the short and fat type. Have you paid for her yet?"

"Not yet, but I've got the cash and I'll get a discount."

"How much?"

"Dollar sixty-nine less three per cent."

"Good Lord!" The bald man leaned forward, aghast. "For that price she must be a pippin. Why, you can buy two hundred average women for that and the market's glutted with them. How old is she?"

"Hundred and nine."

"Oh! That explains it. You're practically getting her right out of the cradle and can teach her whatever you want her to know and see that she doesn't learn anything else. Has she got any mental quirks?"

Fillmore sighed. "She's almost perfect in that respect. Doesn't have to have her mind erased but once every six weeks. Nine power intelligence but she holds it back. That way she doesn't come anywhere near a nervous breakdown oftener than once in six weeks."

"Domestic type?"

"Definitely. Regular homebody. Never been out of the solar system. She's the kind that likes a quiet picnic on Mars and will settle for the moon when Mars is crowded. Besides, she's interested largely in warts and mice. Studies them all the time. Knows how to grow warts on anybody."

"You're a lucky man, Art. Planned the honeymoon yet?"

"Sure. She's going to Venus while I go in the opposite direction. Haven't decided yet where I'll spend that happy time. On one of the planets of the nearer stars, I suppose."

"That's perfect," the bald man said approvingly. "My wife made me stay on earth while she went to the moon. That's too close for comfort. After all, you don't have but one real honeymoon, and in my opinion every man and woman should strive to make it as nearly perfect as possible. I think the government ought to subsidize that sort of thing. Then the happy couple could put more distance between them. Think what bliss could be achieved if the man could afford to go the maximum distance in one direction and send his wife twice that far in the other direction. I mean to say, happiness is next to the ultimate, and if they could be separated so far that no trace of one ever got back to the other — well, just think of it! We would never hear of divorce again."

FILLMORE'S thin angular features darkened. "It is sad to think of the divorces. There's been a dozen in the past half a century. But isn't it because the couples were immature? Some of them married at under eighty years of age, and they insisted on living on the same side of the earth with each other."

"You're pretty young yourself," the bald man put in.

"I'm ninety-six," Fillmore said defensively. "That's plenty old for a man. All of my people matured early."

"And probably died early."

"Yes." Fillmore nodded. "A few of them lived to be nearly five hundred, but they were mostly females. The males usually check out between two and three hundred. Their fourteen power intelligence burns them up."

"Had your mind erased recently?"

"Yesterday. Did it so I could accept Cynthia's proposal without any reservation."

"Cynthia?"

"That's what I call her. Her real name is Xylosh. She found the name Cynthia in one of those books of ignorance unearthed from the ruins of that ancient farm called New York. She asked me to call her by that name. You know how girls are!"

"Sure. They are all very romantic. She may even expect you to be present at the wedding."

Fillmore shook his head and grinned. "She knows better than to spoil things. And I love her too much to let anything like that happen. The ceremony will take place near the earth at the hour when the north pole and the south pole swap places. I'll be somewhere beyond the sun at that time."

"Figuring on any children?"

"Of course. She wants three. We'll have them just before the ceremony."

"That's fine. Gets the dirty work out of the way before marriage and then there's nothing to spoil it. But how are you figuring—"

"That's what I came to see you about. I want to borrow your secretary."

"For what?"

"Well, it's like this. I'm old fashioned. I believe there ought to be some personal contact between a man and his wife before they have children. These laboratory things are so cold-blooded. Mental projections are much better. But there ought to be some personal contact."

"So?"

"So I want to shake hands with your secretary, then she'll shake hands with you and you shake hands with one of your men who's going east and he shakes hands with somebody on the east coast who knows Cynthia's father and that man shakes hands with her father and her father shakes hands with one of his men who shakes hands with his secretary who passes it along until it finally comes to Cynthia. That will give the matter a sort of warmth and personal touch, and then, just before the ceremony, Cynthia and I will mentally project the three children."

"Very touching," the bald man said almost tearfully. "I doubted at first that you and Cynthia actually loved each other, but I see now that any two people so affectionate can't help but love one another. You'll love the children, too."

"Of course. We're going to materialize them fully developed in the government nursery. It will take two or three minutes longer, but we intend to give them a well-rounded education at the beginning. I want the boys to understand the simpler mathematics, such as the theory of relativity and why it is possible to add numerals until you get an answer of zero square. Of course, not everyone can square zero, and it may take ten or fifteen seconds just to teach them that, but I don't want them to grow up to be two or three hours old and still be ignorant. Then, after they've learned those little unimportant things, I'll get down to the business of teaching them everything there is to know. It will take over two minutes and possibly three. Then we'll erase their minds."

"Very ambitious. But what about the girl?"

"Cynthia thinks she ought to learn about warts and I agree. If she learns to grow warts she'll have a first-class female education. I can't think of anything finer in our society. And Cynthia even plans to teach her all about mice."

"It's beautiful," the bald man said. "I'll have my secretary in whenever you're ready."

"Thanks. But not just yet. Chloroform her first. It makes me nervous to be around conscious females. They talk too much."

"Naturally. I don't expect to allow her to speak in your presence. Think I'm a fool without morals? We've got to preserve the conventions. If she saw those three strands of hair on your head she'd swoon. You're the only man in the nation with more than twelve power intelligence who isn't bald. If I didn't know you well I'd think you were effeminate. My wife got a mental glimpse of you once and said you were the handsomest man extant. It's those three strands of blond hair. Even the most beautiful woman in the world doesn't have more than six or seven. I'll bet you really projected those in a big way for Cynthia."

FILLMORE felt the blood rising to his pale cheeks. "I didn't make any special effort," he denied. "Anyway, I'm very presentable. Just under nine feet tall and weigh close to a hundred. My forehead is twelve inches across and eight inches high from the root of the nose. That's better than average. Few men measure more than eleven inches across the forehead."

"True," the bald man admitted "And some persons are troubled with a chin. Fortunately you don't have one. I've got to admit that you are typical of the finer specimens of masculine beauty. Do you ever have a headache?"

"Not since I had my skull cracked. Finest Ducktor in the realm did it with a hammer. Said I needed more room to let my brain expand."

"Of course. I've got a two-inch brain expansion myself. Had to soak my skull in oil until it became malleable enough to allow for the normal brain growth. I've heard of some men having their brain taken out."

"Yeah. Some people are better off without it. But then they have to install an antennae. I wouldn't like that. Which reminds me of something: Got a news flash that scientists were going to awaken a twentieth century man. I don't approve of that sort of thing, but I'm going along to watch. Last time they awakened something from the past it took us quite a while to recover from the mental shock. Had to have my mind erased six times in as many days. Couldn't we do something to stop it?"

"There might be something," said the bald man. "Corson was working on something that would eliminate the past and make everything the present. Only trouble seemed to be that the future got mixed up in it. No. We don't have much chance in that direction—unless—"

"I know what you're thinking," Fillmore said. "I've been working on it myself. Gave it nine seconds solid thought yesterday. If I hadn't been interrupted I might have got it. You're thinking about pure reasoning before the fact."

"Exactly. What are your conclusions?"

"It's possible. The square of nothing equals nothing. When you put nothing times nothing on paper it comes out minus infinity or infinity minus. Thus you have something. Take a mind without a fact and let it confront nothing. Almost at once it will raise nothing to the power of six. It will still have nothing, and so it will head in the other direction until it gets down to infinity minus. That in itself is reasoning *a priori*. Now it has a foundation and from that it can arrive at any conclusion extant, and quite a few that don't exist. Is that what you had in mind?"

"No. I want a conclusion without troubling to confront the mind with even nothing. That is the only way to get pure reasoning."

"If you can give me ten seconds more I'll work it out for you."

"You've already been here thirteen seconds and I'm getting bored. I only get three thousand dollars a day for sitting here, and at slave wages like that I can't put up with too much."

Fillmore nodded. "And prices are away out of reach too. Only the other day I spent six cents for twelve barrels of thousand-year-old whiskey. The world has been aiming at high wages and low prices for the past ten thousand years and we're still slaving and starving. You never told me exactly what you do."

"I work pretty hard. You see, this chair has coils in it that convert heat into Zeta Rays by shortening the wave-length. I sit here for twenty-nine minutes each day, two days a month, and concentrate all my heat through the seat of my pants. It goes through the converter and comes out Zeta Rays in China. Zeta Rays are no good for anything except to convert ordinary rock into gold, so the Chinese pipe it to Russia. Gold, being soft, is good for nothing except to burn ceremoniously in accordance with the ancient religious rites, and so a lot of it is stolen and sold on the gray market to be converted into uranium. Uranium, being useless except for fissionable purposes, is used for fertilizer in the mineral laboratories where iron is grown. Iron is no good for anything except food, and you can't put very much of it in ordinary food, and so it is dissolved into an iron vapor and freed in the atmosphere. Iron vapor gets heavier as it cools, and so it settles on top of the clouds and holds them close to the earth and keeps the warmth of the world from escaping. So, as I sit here and warm this chair, I'm keeping the world warm."

"And getting only three thousand dollars for twenty-nine minutes of that sort of slave labor! Scandalous! I'll bet you can't afford more than a hundred vacations a year. We might as well be back in the dark age of the twentieth century. I've been advocating a one-minute workday for the past decade, one day a month, two months a year. What good is civilization if it doesn't provide something for the poor working man? And people call me a visionary, with Utopian ideas! Bah! If I'm not mistaken, you're the man with the seat of his intelligence in the back of his lap! Right? You're being exploited!"

THE bald man shook his head. "No. It's Corson who's got his intelligence in his back side. Mine is in the soles of my feet, according to Meyer who knows about such things. But Konwell claims the intelligence flows through the bloodstream in all persons."

"Not all," Fillmore contradicted. "But Konwell is right. The brain is merely the antennae. The more blood it gets the more it can express. For instance, in order to concentrate to the full power of fourteen I have to stand on my head. But I can't hang around here all day. Get your secretary in and let me shake hands with her."

"All right. But as a precaution you'd better close your eyes and bring your thoughts down to a six power level. She isn't too bright. It takes her nearly half a second to calculate the distance in inches from here to Andromeda and return via Pegasus—that is, unless you give her a clue to the problem. She's a plain dumbbell but fantastically beautiful. Tall as you are and weighs less than sixty pounds. What a shape! She turned down a billion-dollar contract to dance three minutes in a spot on one of the planets in the Milky Way. Plain dumb! But looks! And the clothes she wears! Dazzling! Imported from Eureka. Must have cost her two-bits or more for one dress with upward of sixty yards of material in it. Made my wife gape. Nearly bankrupted me, my wife did, buying clothes after that. Spent four dollars on her in less than six years. Ten thousand separate items. But, of course, she never found anything like that imported by my secretary. I doubt if there's another in the solar system, and I know there isn't another woman able to afford twenty-five cents for a single dress. I wonder where she gets her money! Her salary here is only seven hundred dollars a day, two days a month. I'll bet she hasn't got a million dollars to her name saved up. Spends every last cent she earns, probably. Ninety cents a quarter she pays for that seventeen room apartment of hers. My wife and I have only eighteen rooms between us, her twelve rooms in China and my six rooms here. Not large either. My six rooms cover only two acres of ground and extend a mere hundred feet in the air. Cramped! I can't afford anything better, not and save anything. I've got less than a billion put aside right now, hardly enough to invest in an enterprise outside the solar system. Poverty! How that secretary of mine lives so high on her pittance, I don't know. I wouldn't be surprised if she isn't consorting mentally with somebody on some planet on the edge of space. Not that I'm narrow-minded. A woman with looks like hers deserves the best, but allowing a man on the edge of space to think about her is going pretty far, and I'm a stickler for the convention.

"Hells bells. I didn't mean to run on like this. But it upsets me to think about her loose morals when I have to work the seat of my pants to the bone over a hot chair in order to earn a bare living. And my wife throwing money around for clothes, and both my boys getting ready to enter college and not in a position to earn anything."

"I can see you're upset. Better have your mind erased."

"I would, but there isn't a good Ducktor closer than Venus. Could find a doctor, of course, but they're unreliable. They style themselves doctors because it sounds like Ducktor. Plain disgrace. Ducktor comes from the word *Quack*. Ages old. Even in the dark ages there were plenty of quacks. They had all sorts of diseases then. Yes, sir. Diseases! Little crawley things working around in their blood and flesh. And these quacks would feed these diseases all sorts of medicine! Finally the diseases up and died. Not having any intelligence to burn them out, the people of those days could live as long as they wished. Or at least that's the way it's figured. Once in a while, about every two or three weeks, just as we erase our minds so we won't burn up too quick, those people would get together and begin killing one another. Think of it! We try to live, but they tried to die. Seems they couldn't die fast enough, so they used a lot of fissionable material and burned up everybody that way. Even that didn't satisfy them, so they used fusing material, which was more deadly, and finally completed everything to their total satisfaction. At least they left very little trace of themselves. Man had to begin all over again from the sea, beginning with the amoeba. I wonder if we're going to wind up like that a million years hence."

"Not likely," Fillmore said. "Besides, you're wrong. Man didn't begin all over again. The amoeba would have worked in another direction, seeing what a mess man made of things. What actually happened was that quite a few people were left after the hydrogen chain was set off. They lived on one of the nearer planets and returned after earth had cooled again. Then they set up things, or so they claimed, very much like they were before, with the exception that they changed their philosophy. Developed their minds first and everything else naturally followed."

"I think it's a mistake," the bald man persisted, "to develop the mind too early. As I mentioned, my two boys are just now entering college. Of course they knew a few things before, such as how to fuel themselves when in the presence of food, and how to walk, and the older one could even speak a few words, and even the younger one could change his own diaper — had been doing it since he was forty-nine—but my wife and I saw to it that they didn't learn too much too fast. That's the reason my people live so long. Don't burn ourselves up in infancy thinking. But that doesn't mean you may not be right in teaching your children, when you have them tomorrow, everything right at the start. With a fourteen power intelligence, your people are by nature compelled to do a lot of thinking, and it's your duty, as a citizen, to begin early. Had any startling thoughts lately?"

FILLMORE sighed. "Just the normal ones. Figured out a simple method, just before dozing off to sleep last night, to transfer this planet to an orbit about another sun. Not that it will be of much use. A sun is a sun and it would take thirty seconds solid thought to improve on it, and I don't know anybody capable of that much sustained thought, and there's not much point in transferring this planet, now that we know how to renew the sun whenever it cools too much."

"But it's interesting," the bald man pointed out. "It gets sort of dull staying in the same old orbit. I'm in favor of moving to another universe. Why don't you bring the matter before the Council?"

"They wouldn't listen. They don't like change. Most of them are aged, and they still think in terms of light and energy. Imagine that in a modern world! Men content to travel at the mere speed of light! Can't get over the idea that breaking through the energy barrier was just like breaking through the sound barrier."

"Was it?"

"Not exactly. But the theory that at the speed of light matter will change to pure energy was just as ridiculous as the theory that matter would disintegrate into sound waves at the speed of sound. They figure light travels at 186,000 miles per second. Perhaps it does in a straight line. I never thought it was worth the trouble of figuring out. But light waves are always at right angle, different from sound waves, and we must come to the conclusion that light does not travel in a straight line, but in a series of curves. While its theoretical speed is 186,000 miles per second, its actual speed is many times that. Thus we have a constant and a variable. If there were only a constant, it would prove out that matter would become pure energy at the speed of the constant. But it does not, for it must achieve the speed of the variable, and that cannot be achieved without traveling at a million different speeds. And even if matter changed to pure energy it must necessarily change again when it breaks through the energy barrier. But those old slow pokes in the council insist that we go on traveling at less than the speed of light. They do not know that a billion miles per second is considered slow in some laboratories. They may know it but they ignore it. Backward! Stupid! Even the ancients were better informed. They conceived varying dimensions, which is a step in the right direction. Actually we know that there is only one dimension and that is the mental dimension with diverse corridors. But in order to learn that, we had to discover, some fifty thousand years ago, upward of two thousand different dimensions. Then we integrated them and found that they all emanated from the mind. It was merely a matter of mathematics and comprehension. And now everything is accomplished by the mind, and in another hundred thousand years we can dispense with our bodies."

"Is that good or bad?"

"Definitely good! We have the itch every few weeks and have to have our minds erased. Nerves! Without bodies we'd be without nerves. That, my friend, is the ultimate quest."

The bald man shook his head. "No. The ultimate quest is the elimination of both the body and the mind. Then we wouldn't have any troublesome thoughts."

"What would be left?"

"Us."

"How do you figure that?"

"I don't know. But you've got a fourteen power intelligence. Get the answer to it and you'll be famous."

"I'll do that. I'll do it right now."

"Not in here. Don't do any concentrating in here. I know how you are when you start thinking. Lightning crackling all around and furniture getting scorched and the building vibrating, and possibly even an earthquake. No, sir. You take your thinking home with you and get inside a thought-proofed vault. You know it's against the law to think above the seven power level out in public where you might start a hurricane or cause snow in the middle of summer."

"Yes. I can see you're right. We've got to get rid of our minds. They are troublesome. I'll go home and figure the whole thing out. And if it's safe I'll pass it along to the council. Good-bye."

"Wait! You want to shake hands with my secretary. I'm going to have her come in."

"That's right. I'd almost forgotten about Cynthia."

"That's another good thing about the elimination of the mind. We won't have to remember anything."

"Well, get her in."

"Right now." The bald man turned his head slightly, glanced at a row of tubes in a panel, selected one and looked at it for a fraction of a second. Instantly the tube glowed brightly and the door of an adjoining office vanished and a woman appeared. Seven strands of jetblack hair on her massive chinless head gave her an ultra feminine appearance, and her eyes, behind their rimless radar equipment were almost as large as a pencil eraser, lending an innocent baby-like air to her lovely features.

She advanced in mincing four-foot strides, parted her tissue-thick lips, and spoke out of a ripe mouth that was fully half an inch wide. The tone of her voice was two octaves above high C, and it so stirred Fillmore with its rich depth that he was compelled to glance at her without opening his eyes. The mental effort was immediately felt by the others, as the temperature of the room increased, and the woman blushed prettily, swaying her lovely nine feet and sixty pounds of pulchritude. She looked at Fillmore, taking in the three strands of blonde hair on his waterbucket head, and swooned. She recovered before she struck the floor, however, and looked to see whether anyone had projected a mental couch for her to fall on. No one had, so she righted herself, readjusted her dress over her twelve-inch bust, patted her seven strands of hair into place, sat down, drew one sixteen-inch foot under her and waited expectantly.

Fillmore was almost on the point of opening his eyes. But he determined to stick to the conventions, because if he gave her any encouragement she might, he knew, try to get chummy with his mind, and that would lead to complications.

"Mr. Fillmore wants to shake hands with you," the bald man explained. "Then you pass it along to me."

"But why doesn't he shake hands with you?" she asked in high C.

The bald man shook his head. "You wouldn't understand about that. But it has something to do with the voltage. Men's voltage multiply, whereas a man and a woman's voltage merely add. If we shook hands we'd burn our brains out. But if you and he shake hands it will merely stimulate you two physically. Nothing dangerous about it."

"It seems immoral," she said.

"I hadn't thought of it that way," the bald man admitted. "But history reveals that men and women even went further than that centuries ago, and never thought anything about it."

The woman coyly lowered her eyes. "If he shakes hands with me," she said softly, "he really should marry me."

"Why?"

"Because I'd probably have a dozen children before tomorrow night."

"Good Lord!" the bald man exclaimed. "That's right. Have you thought about that, Fillmore?"

"No," Fillmore said. "My mind has been turned off for some time. But the hypothesis is reasonable. I'll have to figure out something."

"Not here."

"I've got to. Hold on to your chairs for a moment. I'm going to turn my mind on. Get ready for the shock."

"Not the fourteen power. Don't go over eight or nine."

"Think I'm a fool? I'll keep it down to seven power. Brace yourself, young lady. This is going to be a shock."

THERE was a moment of still silence, then the heat in the room began gradually to rise. In another moment the three blonde hairs were sticking straight up on Fillmore's head and waves of thought were washing about the room in an endless rising tide. The walls creaked and strained and the ceiling sighed upward elastically, giving as it was intended, and a thin gray haze obscured the natural light which was reflected from outside by means of a force field. Fillmore put a cigarette into his mouth, concentrated on the tip of it until it flared into flame, then resumed thinking for a total of two seconds.

"I have it," he said at last. "I'll pull out a strand of my hair, seal it in a ten-ton safe and ship it to Cynthia by armored tube. That is the greatest expression of love any man can possibly make."

"But," the woman broke in, "that is too much. I'm sure she would be satisfied with less."

"No." Fillmore shook his head. "The people of my clan are noted for their courage and chivalry. Should I choose to make the supreme sacrifice for my beloved, who is there to stop me? Call in the reporters. We'll make the announcement right now. My Cynthia shall be honored above women."

"It's beautiful," the woman sighed. "To be loved like that is something every woman dreams of."

"It may cause trouble," the bald man put in. "There was a case once in which a man came within speaking distance of his wife, and the women went wild about it. Some women even insisted on living near their husbands after that, and then the divorces began. You shouldn't do it, Fillmore. Take my word for it, you'll start something that will be hard to stop."

"Maybe you're right," Fillmore admitted. "Men have killed themselves for their wives, but that's nothing. They have given them planets, but that is nothing; they have showered them with stars, and that is very little because there are so many stars. But no man has ever given a woman, up until this time, a strand of his hair, largely because no man had any hair to give. Yes, it would cause trouble. You'd have to grow hair then, and that would cause the race to slip right back into the dark age. This is a problem that calls for fourteen power thought."

"Not here," the bald man shouted.

"Right here," Fillmore insisted. "I'll project a thought-proofed wall about me so that you won't get hurt."

"Well, don't take all day. You've been in this room nearly thirty seconds and haven't accomplished anything yet. Get to work and finish the task. But remember, don't shake this place down or burn it up."

"Relax," Fillmore said.

The bald man and the woman watched the wall grow and then become a sphere. They could easily tell that it was more than six feet thick and harder than a diamond, for it would take every bit of that to restrain Fillmore's full voltage. Besides, he sometimes became radioactive when he turned on full power.

The full matter required one point three seconds. Then the thought-proofed sphere was complete. Then began the dreary wait. Every second seemed like a light year. Five seconds passed, then ten, and still they waited. Then the woman sat bolt upright and uttered an exclamation.

"The sphere is bulging out," she screamed. "It's going to explode."

It was then that the bald man caught the thought beam that came through the sphere: "I've got it! Thinking about hair reminded me of the twentieth century man—he destroyed himself and the world with fissionable hydrogen—only he didn't really destroy himself! Do you get it? He only changed things.

"That's the answer. To eliminate the mind and body we don't destroy, we merely change. Change is the only definite thing anyway. Besides, it will be an interesting thing to cogitate on—the change."

The thought ended on an excited

note. Then the sphere shimmered through the spectrum and with a pyrotechnic display burst outward.

Red, white, blue, purple, and finally black heat shot ten thousand miles through the earth below. The planet shuddered in protest, then disrupted into a gaseous nova. The ultimate quest had succeeded.

Just as in the dark age . . .

THE END

THE SHOOTING LITTLE ROBOT

ANYONE who has seen films taken from the camera guns of fighting planes such as were used in World War II can easily remember the technique of shooting. You see the twin streams of cannon or machine-gun tracer shells converging toward a point hundreds of yards away and then this twin stream gradually "walks" into the target. By judging the angles and distance between the tracers and the target, the pilot made his own corrections and brought his target into range.

This uneconomical method of shooting can't be used in a modern "hot" war. It simply won't work. First of all, jets and rockets move too fast, their guns fire too rapidly, and the rockets and shells must land on the first try. There is no second chance. A modern jet plane fires twenty shells a second. And each gun or cannon has only sixty or a hundred rounds. You can't waste ammunition trying to "stitch" your opponent up and down.

How are you going to make sure you hit him?

The answer is simple — but the technique of getting it isn't. You put a robot brain on the gunsight! This ingenious machine, small and compact amounts to a combined computer and a radar set. The pilot of the six hundred mile an hour jet or rocket makes a crude optical sighting on his target—then the brain takes over. Automatically it allows for windage, speed, angle of approach. It calculates the target's speed, range, and angle of evasion. It corrects itself—all this in tiny fractions of a second. And then when everything is set, it automatically starts the weapons firing, limiting itself to half-second bursts; down comes the target.

As time goes on, and we graduate from the present jets to the coming rockets, it becomes obvious that more and more the presence of the pilot is a hindrance rather than a help. The guided missile, the remote controlled fighting machine, will completely usurp the role of the gunner.

Flesh and blood can't compete with electric circuits, copper and steel—not when time is involved. The robot has to do the high-speed thinking.

Man could get an awful inferiority complex if he didn't stop occasionally and reflect that he's the one who built the brains in the first place. Let's just hope that this is never forgotten, because in the near future we're going to have to live with a lot of thinking machines with mighty powerful electro-mechanical muscles!

It was as if a hole had opened in space, pouring forth the stream of red frogs . . .

IT'S RAINING FROGS!

By MILTON LESSER

George didn't like the idea of little red frogs raining down on him from a clear sky. But a pretty girl falling into his arms was quite another matter!

"We shall pick up an existence by its frogs . . . Wise men have tried other ways. They have tried to understand our state of being, by grasping at its stars, or its arts, or its economics. But, if there is an underlying oneness of all things, it does not matter where we begin, whether with stars, or laws of supply and demand, or frogs, or Napoleon Bonaparte. One measures a circle, beginning anywhere."

—*Charles Fort, LO!*

Illustrated by Ramon Raymond

IT was raining. There wasn't a cloud in the sky, but it was raining. George wished it were raining cats and dogs, but it wasn't. Anything would be better than this. It was raining frogs. Little red frogs.

It was strictly a local rain. The frogs seemed to germinate from a spot somewhere above George's head, and then they spread out and came tumbling down in a cone-shaped area some fifteen feet across. The worst part of it was that George was in the center of the cone.

The frogs fell on him. They seemed to be concentrated most heavily in the center of the cone, and a good percentage of them landed on him—mostly on his head—and then bounced off to fall on the sand. George didn't like it.

He moved. He got up off the sand and ran half a dozen paces closer to the surf, but he still felt the little red frogs striking him. The spot was still directly over his head; George was not sure how high up. He was still the center of the cone.

"Myra! Hey, Myra," George

called his wife. He could see her head bobbing up and down in the waves and the powerful strokes of her arms through the water showed George that she had heard him call. But she would be angry. As soon as he shouted, the frogs stopped falling. First the downpour became a drizzle, and then there were no frogs at all. Myra would be very angry. She was all wrapped up in this new idea of hers, and she would be angry. If he hadn't yelled, more frogs would have fallen—and there's no telling what else, George thought.

The Bikini suit was not in style this year, but Myra wore it because she knew she looked good in it. George watched her run toward him and watched her shake her dark hair loose after she removed the bathing cap. Then he looked at her figure and he knew it was good, so good that he unconsciously felt the spare tire beginning to blossom out around his waist, and he blushed. That was another trouble, he always blushed. Not only that, but he was very fair-skinned. They could spend the entire summer at their seaside bungalow in this secluded area, and Myra would be bronzed like an Indian maiden. But George would turn red and then he would peel. Then he would turn red all over again and then he would peel again. And he had freckles all over.

But he stopped thinking of that now. It was a general consideration. The specific consideration bothered him more: there was one circular area of little red frogs, fifteen feet across. Then there was a trail of little red frogs on the sand, five running steps long. And then there was another fifteen foot circle of them. Most of the frogs were still, but some of them hopped about, and soon the circles had become irregular areas.

Myra came up to him breathlessly. "Oh, George!" she cooed. "You're magnificent, really magnificent. Frogs this time. Little red frogs. You're so—so *Fortean."*

George sighed. He had a lot of friends, and many of them complained because their wives would call this or that thing Freudian. But they had sympathy: a lot of men had wives riding the Freudian merry-go-round. This was worse. To Myra things were *Fortean.* George had seen pictures of this man Fort —a nice enough looking guy with a cherubic face and a ruddy complexion, a turned up nose and big bushy eyebrows. A mild, harmless man. He had passed away; for some twenty years now he had been dead. But he could impress people. His work had impressed Myra.

He thought we're *property,* or things are teleported from one place to another, or we're being fished for, or you can tell a world by its frogs, or science is whacky and word-nutty and sophistic hooey . . . George had heard it all dozens of times. Myra had told him. Myra had told him so much that he thought he knew Fort's philosophy by heart. A lot of ridiculous hogwash—until the rain. How could he call it ridiculous now?

"SEE?" Myra said triumphantly. "See, George? This time it's frogs. Yesterday it was beetles, and the day before, those little birds—and everything was red."

"Maybe they're communists," George suggested feebly.

"Oh——"

"Well, that's as good an explanation as any."

"No, it's not. Red is the predominant color of whatever world they come from, so they're red. Or else it could just be coincidence, but I doubt that. And I told you you were a good catalyst."

"So I'm a good catalyst. So I can make rain. They could have used me back East a few months ago—if they wanted a rain of frogs."

"Or beetles or birds," Myra reminded him.

"Yeah. Beetles and birds, too." George said this matter-of-factly, but then he felt his knees start to tremble. It was the inevitable aftereffect. This was *strange*. It couldn't be happening to him. It never rained that kind of rain, even if Fort had said that it did, and even if Myra believed that Fort was right. How could it rain like that? George knew what caused rain, and by no stretch of his imagination could organic matter be the result. Any sort of organic matter. And least of all little red frogs. He always associated frogs with mud—and the idea of little red frogs coming from the sky was too incredible to consider.

But there were the frogs on the beach.

George stroked the sand gingerly with the toes of one foot, clearing frogs away until he had room to sit down. He sat.

One of the little red frogs jumped into his lap, and he stood up again—so fast that he almost upended Myra.

"My gosh, George. You may be a good catalyst, but after that you're hopeless. That's where I come in."

George was sorry he had decided to play along with his wife. She had given him a test, and that part he enjoyed, for all he did was shoot dice for several hours. Something about psychokinesis, Myra said. And George scored high. So high that Myra had cried: "You're positively Fortean!"

And then had come the birds, the beetles, and the frogs. All red.

"Listen," George said. "This is the last time. This is positively the last time."

"The last time? Last time for what?"

"The last time that I let you use me as a—a catalyst. I can't go around making it rain like that. We're in a deserted spot out here, so it isn't too bad. But what if this happened when people were around? What then?"

"Silly, why do you think we came to this bungalow for the summer? And besides, even if people were around, why would they think *you* caused the rain? If you insist on calling it rain."

George did not like the way she said *you*. It was as if he didn't amount to much—but she always spoke to him like that. He knew he was no world-beater. He had an adequate job and he made an adequate salary, but he just didn't stack up like some of the men he knew. Or some of the men Myra knew. It always got him angry when she said *you* that way.

"What do you mean, why should they think I caused the rain? Who else can cause it, that's what I want to know? Who else can cause it?"

She smiled, and if it was a smile of triumph, George pretended not to notice it. "That's what I mean," she said, putting her arms around his neck. "You're so wonderful. Only you can cause it. Let's go into the house, George."

He grunted and he disentangled her arms. Then he took her hand and walked back across the sand to the house. And he held his head very high so he wouldn't have to look at all the little frogs on the beach.

THEY sat in the living room and the sun was setting, throwing long shadows across the room through the big picture window. George sipped his bourbon and then he put his glass down. Two drinks on an empty stomach always put that dreamy feeling in his head. He wanted to get up and pour himself another, but it was so pleasant just sitting here and thinking of nothing that he decided against it.

"You're ready now," Myra told him. "Oh, you're really perfect now. Remember, George, just think of nothing. Don't think of a thing. Lean back, relax, and keep your mind a blank. It shouldn't be too hard."

There was that undertone of scorn again, but now George didn't feel like doing a thing about it. She was right: it wouldn't be too hard. He had had his two drinks of bourbon, and now he would just sit back and relax, like Myra told him. Besides, he had nothing to worry about. It couldn't very well rain anything inside the house.

"It's just like the poltergeists," Myra was saying, but George hardly heard her. "There are so many cases of poltergeist phenomena on record, of the little mischievous ghosts who throw dishes or stones or who cause pointless little accidents. And in each case, there's a catalyst. Usually it's a little child, and more often than not, a girl, but that isn't always the case. The important thing is, there has to be a catalyst."

"That's me," George said proudly.

"Yes, that's you. My George, the

best damn catalyst that ever lived." Myra had had her bourbon, too. "You know, science always explains away the poltergeists, but they do a pretty awful job of it. A lot of people aren't satisfied. Like Fort. Like me."

Was that a compliment? Was any of it a compliment? George thought so, but he couldn't be sure. His mind was fading into a pleasant haze of deep red, like the sunset. His eyes were opened and he was looking into the sunset, and that's why he saw the deep red. But then he noted a fact which would have startled him, only it didn't now. He was tired and he closed his eyes and still the deep red persisted, stronger than ever. It didn't startle him because he was too perfectly relaxed, and because the deep red was so soothing . . .

"Were you calling me?" the voice said.

GEORGE jumped up. He thought he had heard the voice, but he couldn't be sure. Now the sun had set completely and a heavy dusk settled over the room.

"What did you say, George? George, did you ask me anything?"

George said no, he didn't, and he got some slight satisfaction from the fact that Myra's voice sounded frightened. But then a slow chill crept up his spine and spread all over his body. Myra had heard the voice too.

"Well, were you calling me? Come, come, I haven't got all day, and if you weren't calling me, then I'll go home."

George gulped, and he heard Myra choke off a little whimper in her throat. Then George smiled. Hell, one of their friends from down the beach had come, and he decided to act mysterious here in the darkness. It was Andy. Andy would play practical jokes like that. Andy, the life of the party.

George strode jauntily to the light switch. "Hah, hah, had us fooled for a minute, Andy old boy. And nope, the answer is that we didn't call you. But you're always welcome here, you know that. Come on and join us in some bourbon."

His hand was on the light switch now, and he flicked it up. The room was bathed in the pale white of the flourescent lamps, and George turned around to say hello to Andy.

He stood in the center of the room. He stood there regarding George with a half smile on his lips, a playful smile. You couldn't tell his age and there was nothing special about his features. But the half smile remained on his lips like something permanent. He was definitely not Andy.

"As you can see, I'm not this Andy person."

"No. You're not," said George.

"Now, then. Who called me? Which one of you called me?"

Myra's voice was husky. The way it sometimes was at night, after a few drinks. The way George liked it. Only now she was scared. "I guess we both—called you."

"I wouldn't have come myself, of course, except that the message was so urgent. The call has never come out that strong before. I'm not just speaking about that from memory, of course. I'm king now but I haven't been around that long. There are records—and your call is twice as strong as any of the others. I could have sent an assistant, naturally, but I figured if the call was this strong I'd come myself."

HUMOR him, George thought. He's just a nut who came in off the beach. Only the reasoning was lousy. It stank. The door was locked and the big picture window was locked from the inside, so he could not have come in off the beach. George sighed.

"This is silly," the man was saying. "You put through such an urgent call that I come here myself. Then, when I arrive, no one will tell me what for."

"I know!" Myra cried. "You're from the world of the red frogs."

"What say?"

"I said you're from the world of the red frogs. You rained."

"Yes, I reign. I've been reigning for eleven years now, ever since my father died. Actually, though, it's open to question. While I'm the titular head, there's my wife to consider. She does a lot of reigning herself. In fact, she'll be pretty angry when she learns I answered the call myself. Below my dignity or some such thing. She always wants me to be dignified, but that's stupid, because she's anything but dignified herself. You know, I often think it isn't any fun to be king."

"That's nice," George said.

"I mean," Myra said, "you *rained*. Rained—r-a-i-n-e-d, like the frogs."

"Oh, the frogs. Yes, they would come through first, of course. Something about making sure the co-ordination is right. A messenger could go straight through at once, but that would be dangerous, and if the co-ordination were off, he'd be a sorry mess. Frogs or bugs or sometimes birds, we send anything through to make sure. Anyway, what do you want?"

"Now that you mention it, I don't know. I guess we don't want anything. We were just experimenting," Myra explained.

"Experimenting? Will you stop kidding? With a call as strong as that, experimenting? I wasn't born yesterday, sister. Look, don't be afraid of my wife. She doesn't know where I've gone and it will be some time before she can find me, so tell me the truth."

"That's the truth. I knew we'd get something, but I didn't know what. We got you. My husband is very psychokinetic."

The man shrugged. "He hardly looks it."

"Oh, don't let George fool you.

He's potent that way."

"That's me," George said. "I'm a terrific catalyst. Ask Myra."

"He is," Myra said.

"Well, then I see it was all a mistake. Do you think he could get me back?"

"Of course he could get you back. You said yourself this was the strongest call on record. Get him back, George."

George smiled. He was beginning to like this. It all depended on him. The man with the enigmatic smile knew exactly what was going on, Myra knew to some extent what was going on, George knew almost nothing of it, but everything depended on him. "Why should I?" he demanded. "He only just came, and I'm not in any hurry to send him back."

"Please," the man said, and for the first time the smile began to fade from the corners of his mouth. "It was all a mistake, and now I'd better get back home before my wife finds out."

George felt cocky. "Well, it was your mistake, not mine, and I don't feel like sending you back yet. So I guess you'll stay right here."

"You're not serious?"

"Serious? You bet I'm serious. I don't even know where I'm supposed to send you, but I'm not going to. At least not for a while yet."

"Now, look. You've got to send me back. I'm the king."

"Send him back, George. You don't know what you're playing around with. Send him back."

"No."

"I'm the king."

"Send him back, George."

George got up and took a long drink of the bourbon. His stomach was still empty, except for the previous bourbon, and the drink sent a warm glow through him. "No," he said.

THEY sat there in the living room, the three of them. George on the sofa, Myra on a straight-backed chair, and Arl cross-legged in the middle of the floor. The king's name was Arl, he had told them that. And then afterwards, he was silent. He was sullen, and George smiled. He was in trouble and he did not know what to do and it all depended on George.

"Listen, George," Arl was trying another angle. "Maybe if I tell you what this is all about, then will you send me back?"

"I doubt it, but maybe I will. Just a slight, improbable maybe. But I guess you're grasping at straws now. Say on."

"Better send him back, George," Myra said. "I got you into this and you don't know what it's all about, but you better do what he says."

"Do *you* know what it's all about?"

"No, I don't. But I know more than you, and I know that you better not horse around."

"Well, I'll listen to what he has

to say. But I better tell you now that I doubt if I'll send him back. I didn't really call him, you did. Now *you* send him back."

"If I could I would. I don't want to play around like this. It can cause trouble. If he loses his temper, George—well, just don't say I didn't warn you."

"Unfortunately," Arl admitted, "it takes me a long time to lose my temper. It never used to be that way. But Narka—that's the queen—has tamed me. A king should not be so impetuous, she told me, only she's as impetuous as hell. That's the trouble. She's all the time telling me to do things which will make me more polite, more refined, more cultured—none of which she does herself. The result is that I've become more of a figurehead, and she's the real power. It's regrettable."

"That's not an uncommon situation," George assured him. "But just what are you titular king of?"

"Then you do want to hear my story!"

"Yeah, yeah. I said I wanted to hear it. I didn't say I'd do something about sending you back, but go ahead and tell me if it will make you happy."

"Okay. I'll begin with a question. Do you know anything about the fourth dimension?"

GEORGE was silent, but Myra said: "I know all about the fourth dimension."

"You just think you do. Actually, you don't know a thing about it. A lot of fuzzy thinking here in the world of three dimensions, but you really don't know a thing about it."

"Oh," said Myra.

"You tell her, Arl, old boy," George said. "You tell her. That guy Fort didn't know what he was talking about."

"Fort? Fort? Oh—yes he did. He knew *what* he was talking about. But he didn't know how or why. This is a world of three dimensions, right?"

"Uh-huh."

"Well, let's assume you had a world of two dimensions. Of length and breadth, but no thickness. How would you get a world of three dimensions?"

George said, "Search me," but Myra went into a long explanation which George didn't understand at all.

When she finished, Arl shook his head. "Just what I thought. A lot of fuzzy thinking. Unfortunately, you're way off the beam. It's really simple. You have a world of two dimensions — length and breadth, and all you have to do to get a world of three dimensions is extend that world in a new direction—perpendicular to the first two. That direction is up or down, as the case may be. Either way, it's a direction at right angles to the first two, and the result is a world of three dimensions, this world."

George said he understood. "But

that doesn't mean I'm going to send you back," he added.

Arl was all wrapped up in his explanation, and he ignored the remark. "Now, then. The same situation applies. The same relation exists between a world of three dimensions and one of four. You merely extend the three dimensions out in a direction at right angles to them—a direction which is perpendicular to length, breadth and thickness, and the result is a world of four dimensions. That's my world."

George was feeling chipper. "Well, a pat on the backside for you," he said. "Now I suppose you want me to send you back?"

ARL waved his hand. "No. I'm not finished. Let's go a step further. If a world of two dimensions existed—a whole world spread out perfectly flat on this table, with no dimension other than length or breadth, a flat world—if that world existed, do you realize all the power you, as a three dimensional being, would have over it?"

George said that he didn't.

"Well, suppose something was enclosed in a square on that table. Just four lines, a square. That would be the equivalent of a cube in this world—say, of a safe. Say there was something in that square that the people of the flat world wanted to get out. But the square was locked. It was just four lines, forming an enclosed space, but because there was no such thing as up or down in that world, they couldn't get over those lines and get out what they were looking for. It was utterly inaccessible.

"Now, then. You're a three dimensional creature. All you'd have to do is reach down, pick the item up, transport it through the third dimension, and put it down again outside the square. You would have done the impossible. You would have taken something out of an utterly inaccessible place and put it elsewhere. Mysteriously.

"So, just change the situation a bit. A four dimensional being would have the same power over this three dimensional world. He could make things appear and disappear easily, simply by transporting them through the fourth dimension. And that, my friend, explains everything strange and unreal and impossible which this man Fort reported. It was simply the intervention of a four dimensional being. One of my subjects. When the call comes through, your people are not even aware that they give it. But when it does come through, we answer. And here the call was the strongest on record. I'm the king and I came through myself. But we can't come through and we can't go back without the call. That's you, George, and it was all a mistake. Now will you send me back?"

George smiled. He enjoyed this situation. He thoroughly enjoyed it, and he watched Myra's face turn white as he said one word:

"No."

"BE reasonable, George. If you don't send me back, there'll be trouble. I won't tell you what kind of trouble, but don't say you were not warned in advance."

"Well, maybe you ought to tell me. What kind of trouble?"

"Narka trouble," Arl said, and George could see that the man's hands were trembling. "When my wife finds out, she'll be mad. When Narka's mad, she's very mad. And not just at me—she'll be on the warpath with you, too. She'll come here and——"

"How can she come here, without your call?"

"Oh, she'll find a way. Getting back is the difficult part. Please, George."

"No. No, I don't think so. Myra started all this, not me. I told her to stop but she didn't want to. Now I think I'll let the two of you stew in your own juice for a while. You can't blame me. In a sense, I'm just an innocent bystander who happens to be a top-flight catalyst. But this could be amusing. I'll just let things stand."

Arl turned to Myra. "Myra, do you want me to go back?"

"Yes. Yes, I suppose so. You know more about this than we do, but my husband can be so obstinate——"

"I'm not being obstinate. This was all your idea, and now I want to see what happens."

Arl said, "There'll be quite a mess. Not only will Narka be angry with us, but the call will be coming through from all over, and none of our subjects can go over without my permission. You know what that means?"

George asked him what.

"That means that there'll be a lot of situations where poltergeists should have appeared, sort of like the old *deux ex machina* of your early literature, only they won't. That, my friend, will cause a mess."

George laughed. " I don't know. I've known a lot of people to get along well enough without your poltergeists. Everyone I've ever known, in fact. All my life."

Myra shrugged helplessly. "Honest, Arl, I'm sorry. It's just that George is so ordinary."

George scowled. He had been on the verge of relenting. He definitely had been on the verge of relenting. But that did it. He wouldn't relent now.

"Can't you make him?" Myra demanded.

"No. That's the difficulty. I can't. The caller must either be unaware or willing, and your husband is neither. There isn't a thing I can do about it until he changes. Ordinarily, I could do many things so that he'd see it our way—but that would necessitate popping in and out of the fourth dimension, and without George's help, I can't do that. It all rests with George."

"Well, maybe we can *make* him cooperate."

"How do you mean, make him?"

"I mean physically. There are two of us and one of him and maybe we can make him."

MYRA advanced, and Arl was a little slower, but presently he got the idea, and he too came toward George. "Stay back," George warned. "Keep away from me or I'll never change my mind, and then you'll be stuck here forever."

"He's right," Arl said.

"No, he's not. We can make him. We can force him to change his mind."

Myra was so close now that George could reach out and touch her. He backed up a step. Myra was young and strong and she was athletic. Every curve of her lithe body was deceptively strong and beautiful at the same time, and George was developing that spare tire around his middle. It was small but it was there and George knew he was anything but athletic. He did not want to fight with Myra, especially when Arl, who was a head taller than George, would be helping her. It definitely was unwise.

Myra's first attack was merely speculative. She pushed George to see if he would fight back. He backed up two or three steps, and then he was sitting on the sofa.

Arl was much less speculative. He reached down and yanked George to his feet. Then he began to shake George.

"Hey, stop it!" George's voice sounded like a rattle.

"We won't stop until you change your mind," Myra told him, and to show that she was serious, she poked her fist in George's stomach, hard. He felt the air *woosh* out of his lungs, and then he was sitting on the sofa again. At another time he might have thought this was getting monotontous, but he didn't think so now. When Arl picked him up again, he tried to cringe away, but Arl held him tight.

He butted his head at Arl, and the king stumbled back and away from him, losing his grip on George's shoulders. George didn't back up; he stalked after the king, and when he reached him he balled his right fist and struck out with it.

THE contact was a bit painful, but George was happy with the result. Arl stumbled and fell. He was all stretched out on the floor, and he didn't try to get up.

"I did that," George said.

"You stinker. My own husband, and what a stinker you turned out to be."

"Now, my dear——" George began, sure of himself. But the words caught in his throat. Myra threw herself at him, bodily, and George sat down. He was sitting on the floor and then he was down flat and Myra was sitting on his chest, and those two hammers hitting his face were her fists. They hurt.

Myra and George had had fights before. George was not a violent man, he knew that. He always wanted to settle things with words, and whenever Myra lost her temper he would make it a point not to be around because he thought she could beat him, and if she did that once, there'd be no living with her. But now he couldn't make it a point not to be around because Myra was sitting on his chest and he couldn't get up.

George heaved up and over, and he felt Myra roll off him. Then he sat up and he pulled Myra across his knees. She struggled, but he held her down with one hand and with the other he did the only thing that a husband should do in a case like this. He spanked her. At first she was volubly indignant, but then she began to whimper, and George didn't stop until she was howling. He pushed her away and stood up, smoothing the crease in his trousers. Arl's head was propped up on one elbow now, and Arl had a dark discoloration around one of his eyes, but the look he gave George was one of pure admiration.

"I wish I had the nerve to do that to Narka," he sighed. "That's what she needs. I can see it now. That's what she needs."

George strode around the room jauntily. "You can if you want to, Arl. Just because you're a king doesn't mean that you can't." Then he turned to Myra. She was just getting up, blowing her nose in a dainty little handkerchief.

At first George couldn't quite fathom the look she gave him. She was angry, of course. But she was something more than a n g r y. "George," she said, and his name came out in a long sigh, and he knew that for the first time he had made a conquest of his wife.

"I'll be in our city apartment," he told her. "If you want me, that's where I'll be. And I guess you both realize my mind is made up. Arl will remain here until I'm good and ready to send him back. Good night."

George went outside, got into the car, drove it down the dirt road to the highway, and headed for the city.

He was whistling.

GEORGE sat on his stool at the bar and ordered a straight bourbon. He had changed his mind about going to his apartment immediately. Instead, he had gone to this bar. He had something to celebrate. Something told him that this business was far from finished yet, but he didn't care. It was incredibly fantastic, but he relished the prospect of more dealings with King Arl, and with Myra, too.

He lifted the tumbler of bourbon to his lips and sipped it. But then he set the glass down on the bar, hard, and it toppled over. Something had plunked on his head.

"Hey," the bartender roared "That's good bourbon. You just spilled it all over. Now you'll say it's my fault and you'll want another."

"No," George said absently. "Forget it."

Something plunked on his head again. He put his hand up and plucked at his hair. The thing was wet and slimy. It was a little red frog. George held it out in front of him and then he placed it down on the bar.

"Now, look," the bartender was getting angry. "You think you're a wise guy or something? Who ast you to bring them little animals in here? This is a respectable joint, and I got my customers to think of."

George said he was sorry. Plunk! Another frog came down on his head. He felt it hop off, and then he saw it alight on the bartender's shoulder.

"Yoiks! Cut it out, bud! I'm warning you, cut it out." He was a little fat man with a bald head and his face was all red, almost like the frogs. "You stop that, bud. I don't wanna play games with you."

George said he was sorry again and he watched the bartender brush at the frog with one hand. It landed on the bar then it jumped twice and landed on the hand of a customer two stools down from George.

It was a lady but she let out a very unladylike howl and stalked out of the bar.

"She went out without paying her bill!" the bartender told George. "So you owe me for it. Three-fifty."

George wondered about this. Arl said he was helpless without George's call, so this couldn't be Arl's work. Someone wanted to come through from the four dimensional world, and that someone had been receiving the call from George. He had been sipping his bourbon, minding his own business, yet he had given the call. He had been unaware of it but he had been giving it, and that could be embarrassing. As it was now.

"Three-fifty," the bartender said. "Three-fifty or I'm gonna force myself to call a cop."

George handed over the money and left hurriedly.

HE sat near the front of the trolley car, hoping that no more frogs would fall. He could have walked home, but that would have taken much longer, and there might be more frogs. This way, he was taking a chance that they wouldn't fall in the trolley car, and, if they did, he'd ignore them.

Three more stops and George would be home. He closed his eyes and sighed contentedly. He would be safe then. He didn't want any more frogs falling in public. Not while he was around.

Something soft but firm pressed his lap, and George opened his eyes. He yowled. He couldn't help it. It was only a little yowl, but several people looked at him. And then they began to yowl, especially one buxom middle-aged lady. "It's indecent," she cried. "Utterly, thoroughly and obnoxiously indecent. Somebody call a policeman at the next corner."

The driver looked in the mirror, astonished, and nodded. George blinked his eyes, but when he opened them she was still there. She sat in his lap and she was very beautiful. She didn't have a stitch of clothing on.

"Please," George pleaded. "Go away! Please go away. Go away and put some clothing on and then come back if you want, but not like this!"

"You sent for me. You were in such a hurry you didn't even give me a chance to dress. Now you want to send me back. What's the matter, don't you like me?"

George felt the flush spread over his face. "Please," he said again. "Go away. Everyone's staring at us."

"Okay," she pouted. "Okay. I'll go away. Just put that call out again and I'll be able to do it." Her hair was long and billowing, the color of copper, and it tickled George's face. "But I'll be back. Don't you worry. I'll be back. And —if you see Arl—tell him I'm looking for him. Just wait till I get my hands on him, you just wait—"

George blinked. The lovely creature was gone.

He had not been aware of the fact that the trolley had stopped. Now a policeman stood in the aisle next to him.

"How'd you do it, pal? Come on, how'd you do it? I saw the girl and she was naked as Lady Godiva. Just try to explain your way out of this one . . . "

"It was utterly indecent," the buxom woman said. "I was going to visit my little grandchildren, but how can I after that? How can I?"

"That," George told her acidly, "is your problem."

"A wise guy, too, eh?" The officer was belligerent.

"It's not too difficult to explain, officer. Something like hypnotism. Something very much like it. It's called psychokinesis, I think."

"Psychokinesis, psychoshminesis. You just come on down with me and explain it to the sergeant."

George went with him and he explained it to the sergeant, but it did no good. The sergeant listened and then his face got very red. He had a thick neck and his uniform collar was too tight for it, and his neck got all red, too. He told George he could cool off his mental powers in jail overnight and pay a twenty-five dollar fine.

. . . They gave George breakfast early in the morning. It wasn't very good, but he was hungry and he ate all of it. Then he hurried out of his cell and left the stationhouse. The whole cell was filled with little red frogs, and he could hear the patrolmen bellowing as he left, but he hurried down the stairs and flagged a taxi.

HE tried to relax in the apartment, but it was no good. He thought of the girl who had materialized in his lap, and he knew she was Narka. He wished she would come back because he wanted to see what would happen when she met Arl. And there were other reasons, too. He wondered if she would be wearing clothing. And the next thought, of course, was a logical one: what kind of clothing would a fourth dimensional queen wear?

At ten the doorbell rang.

He opened the door, and Myra came in. Behind her was Arl, and George had never seen anyone so frightened as Arl looked.

"What the hell is wrong with you?" George demanded.

"Nothing — yet. I just read in the newspaper about you and the naked girl in your lap — mass hypnotism, the report said. But we both know it wasn't. It was Narka. Where is she?"

George said not to worry because she had gone back to the world of the red frogs, and then Myra grabbed his shoulder and spun him around sharply. She often did that when she was angry and wanted his attention, and George had never done anything about it. He didn't do anything this time, either. He just looked at her, and she removed her hand from his shoulder. Her face was very white when she spoke.

"What was she doing in your lap, George?"

"What do you think she was doing?"

"That's what I'm asking you. Please, George. I'm sorry about yesterday. I don't know what got into me. I never should have tried to hit you. A wife has no business trying to hit her husband."

"Nuts," George said. "You just thought you could get away with it, that's all. Now that you know you can't, you're trying to say you're sorry. Nuts."

Then he looked at Arl fondly. Arl was to thank for all this. If it hadn't been for Arl, he would still be henpecked. Myra didn't look like the type that would henpeck her husband, but George smiled ruefully at this thought. She was the type, and she did it every chance she got. Only she wouldn't do it anymore. Arl had been *that* catalyst. "Arl," George said, "I could love you like a brother."

"What about my wife?" Arl still wanted to know. "Where's my wife?"

"I told you, she went back. For some clothing, I think."

"Then she was sitting in your lap with no clothing on!" Myra said indignantly.

"Yes, she was."

"What was she doing in your lap with no clothing on?"

"You asked me that once."

"Please, George. What!"

"She was sitting," George said. He winked at Arl, but Arl only shuddered. Now *there* is one henpecked king, George thought.

Then he stood up expectantly. A frog had plunked down on his head.

THE look of expectancy on George's face faded. He waited, but there was nothing of Narka. No more frogs fell.

"That was tentative," Arl said.

"What do you mean, tentative?"

"I mean a tentative breakthrough into this dimension. Someone changed his mind. But I shouldn't say someone and I shouldn't say his. It was Narka." He was trembling.

"Get a hold on yourself, Arl. This is not the end of the world."

"You don't know Narka."

"You've just got to know how to handle women, that's all. Let them think they have the upper hand, and you're through. Just show them who's boss, that's all."

Myra seemed on the verge of snorting. But instead she smiled brightly at Arl. George is certainly right."

"Of course I'm right. Buck up, Arl."

"Well, it's easy to say. But I can't."

George snorted himself and went for the bourbon bottle. He had never taken a drink before mid-afternoon in his life, but now he figured a lot of changes had to be made. Necessary changes.

"I have a terrific idea," Arl said.

George didn't think it would be terrific, but he said: "What's that?"

"Well, you have to put the call through, you know. So, why don't you just — don't?"

"Eh? Say that again."

"Don't put the call through. Don't put it through and Narka won't be able to come."

Myra nodded her head vigorously. "That sounds like a fine idea," she said.

George said, "It stinks. It so happens I want to see Narka again."

"After you see her, you'll be sorry. I'm not saying you can't handle women, George. Don't misunderstand me. Myra is a spitfire a lot like the Queen, but you certainly can handle Myra. I don't mean that."

George was pleased. "Of course. What do you mean?"

"Well, Narka is — "

HE stopped talking. Something fell to the floor at George's feet, and he stopped to pick it up. He held it in his palm — a necklace of flawless pearls, worth a small fortune. He held it in his hand, not knowing what to do with it.

"That's what I mean," Arl said.

"Oh, it's beautiful," Myra cooed. "Is it for me, George? Where did you get it?" Then she pouted. "It's not for — that Narka, is it? It's for me, isn't it, George?"

"That's what I mean," Arl said

again. "Narka cannot resist the impulse to steal everything she likes in this dimension. She simply takes what she likes, and I know several cases in which one of your three dimensional men went to jail for a series of robberies committed by the Queen."

"That's ridiculous," George said. "How can she steal so many things?"

Arl shook his head. "You're forgetting the relationship between the three and four dimensional worlds again. Remember, it's like you and that square on the table. How would you get a necklace out of that square without crossing any of its lines?"

"Why — why, I'd simply lift the necklace up and then put it down on the other side of one of the lines."

"Exactly. That's what Narka's doing. She sees what she likes, lifts it up out of your three dimensional existence, momentarily carries it through the fourth dimension, and puts it down here. When she has all she wants, she'll come for her booty, then I'm afraid she'll take me home with her. Only she'll be very mad. She won't speak to me for a week — she'll do other things, bad things. I wish you had never called me, George."

Something went *plop*, and George saw a small velvet cushion on the floor. Like a pin cushion. And pinned to it were a number of jeweled brooches. George did not know too much about jewelry, but he didn't have to be an expert to know that these were valuable pieces. Even if he didn't know it himself, he could tell by the way Myra sighed. Myra would not sigh at imitations.

GEORGE laughed. "Now I know how Ali Baba must have felt after he said 'Open, Sesamee.' "

Myra nodded, but she hardly heard him. She walked from one treasure to the next, as each new one plunked down on the floor or the chairs or the tables. She was running, soon, with excited little gasps, feeling the jewels with her hands, caressing them, holding them to her throat and letting them caress her, raising them to the window so she could see the sun shine on them.

Arl said wearily, "I have seen this many times before. It's always the same the first time. Narka collects the treasure and someone here in this three dimensional world sees the treasure come in. The result is always the same. It's quite a sight the first time. Narka has sufficient jewelry here to buy this city."

"Well, it doesn't affect me that way," said George. But he only said it — he didn't feel it at all. This interdimensional travel was the answer to all his dreams. You saw something you wanted, you lifted it out into the fourth dimension, you came back with it to the world of three dimensions — and that's all there was to it.

"Don't tell me you're not thinking the same thing they all have thought in the past," Arl said. "I know you are. Everyone does. But I warn you, George: that way lies madness."

He could be a king, George thought. Not a titular king like Arl, but the real thing — a king in the true sense of the word, the old sense of the word. He'd want something — anything — and it would be his. Just like that.

"No more treasure," Myra said. "It isn't raining anymore."

George looked. The room was abrim with precious stones, and apparently Narka had enough for this trip. She had stolen a king's ransom — more than that. And there was that word again: with this power, George could be a king.

"No," he said.

"What's that?"

"Um, nothing, Arl. Nothing. Just thinking out loud." He did not want to be a king, not that way. Human values were too high, and he had moved on the straight and narrow path too long. Not that there was anything wrong with the straight and narrow path. Suddenly he liked it — it was very important to him, and although he remembered Narka as he had seen her, naked and beautiful, he thought of her now only as a cheap thief. The wild urge had gone—this was not the way to kinghood.

ABRUPTLY, Narka was there. One moment there were only the three of them and the treasure. The next, she stood next to George, and when she materialized, she was leaning on George's arm.

"I'm back," she said.

She wore a tunic, only it was more transluscent than a tunic had a right to be. But George didn't mind. He didn't mind in the least. It was unfortunate, though, that he was so interested in the effects Narka's arrival would have on Arl. He looked at the woman only for a moment, and then he turned his eyes to her husband.

Arl was trembling. He looked ordinary compared with Narka. He wore what could have passed for a white linen suit, and it fit well. With that enigmatic smile, he could have been a good looking man, but right now he was trembling, and his mouth hung open.

"Narka — " he said.

"Don't you 'Narka' me. You know I didn't want you to come, but you came anyway. Just wait till I can get you home alone. Wait till I get you — "

"Wait is right," said George. He gestured to the jewelry about the room. "Right now there's another matter, a more important matter. What about your, ah, trophies?"

"What about them?" She gave George's arm a little squeeze, and George liked the feeling. But he saw Myra wince. "What about them? Why, nothing. I'll just take them home with me, that's all. I have a whole section of the palace filled with them."

"No you won't," George said.

"Don't be silly. Who's going to stop me?"

"I am."

She leaned more heavily on George's arm, and she looked up at him with her big round eyes. "No you're not."

"No? How are you going to get back unless I help you?"

"You'll help me. I'll leave some of these jewels here with you. Name any three items and they're yours."

Myra suggested, "That brooch, and that — "

"Shut up," said George.

Narka frowned. "Are you going to let him talk to you like that?"

Myra looked at George. "Y-yes," she said. "But please stop holding on to his arm like that. If George says you take all those things back where they belong, then you'd better do it. I — I think George knows best."

"He does," Arl assured his wife.

"You shut up, Arl. I'll attend to you later." Narka made no move to release George's arm. She leaned closer to him and stood on her tiptoes. Then she kissed him. George liked it — he liked it a lot. This Narka was quite a girl, even if she was a crook.

"Now, George," she said, "send us back."

"No." George pulled his arm away, and Narka was leaning over so far that she almost fell.

"Hah," Myra said.

Narka smiled. "Arl," she said, "pick up the jewelry, and we'll get started."

"How can we get started if George won't send us back?"

"Just be quiet and pick up the jewelry."

OBEDIENTLY, Arl went about the room, gathering the treasures in his arms. It took a few minutes, and George stood by patiently, smiling. Finally, arms full, Arl nodded to his wife. "That's all, dear."

Narka looked at George. "Now, send us back."

George shrugged. "I said no, and I wasn't kidding. You take all that jewelry back where it belongs, and I'll send you back. Not before."

For a long moment, Narka looked at him. "You know," she said, "I think I will get you in trouble. Yes, I think I will. You definitely deserve it."

The apartment was on the fourth floor, near the corner. Narka strode to the window and opened it. Behind her, George looked out. Down on the corner directing traffic was a cop.

"He's a law officer, isn't he?" Narka demanded.

George nodded, and before he could stop her, Narka took two brooches and a necklace from the pile in Arl's arms, called to the policeman, and, when she had caught his attention, threw the jewelry down to him.

"Oh, no . . . " Myra moaned.

George shut the window. In a few minutes the policeman would be in the room. He'd see a room full of jewelry, and he'd receive reports of all the thefts in the past few minutes, the incredible number of thefts in so short a space of time, and though he would not know how it was done, he would blame George. He would definitely blame George.

A few minutes . . .

"You shouldn't have done that," George said.

Narka stuck her tongue out at him. It was very unladylike, even less queen-like. "No?"

"No." George reached out and pulled Narka to him. He saw the look of triumph on her face.

"George," she said coyly.

Holding her arm and retreating to a big chair, George sat down. Because he was still holding her, Narka sat on his lap, and from there it wasn't hard for him to turn her over. He did and then she got the idea, but it was too late. She struggled and she writhed but she couldn't do a thing about it.

"What you need," George told her, "is a good three-dimensional man to take care of you."

"Let me up or I'll — I'll beat you."

"You'll *what?*"

"I'll beat you. Ask Arl, he's a man, but I beat him. When I get him home, I will beat him."

GEORGE lifted his hand, but Arl caught it in mid-air. "Wait, George. I think I am learning." Arl was still trembling, but he attempted a smile. "I think I am learning."

George smiled and got up. Arl sat on the chair next to his wife. Men could be henpecked just so long, George thought — even in the fourth dimension, it couldn't go on forever.

But Arl's smile was uncertain, he was trying to bolster his courage with it, and Narka stared grimly, certainly. Suddenly, she and Arl were locked together, struggling. George breathed hard. The cop would be here in another minute or two, but he had to let Arl fight his own battle. A king could not be a king in name only, and he had tried to show Arl the way.

Narka wrestled Arl to the floor and held him there, next to the remainder of the jewelry. Arl began to moan, and then Narka laughed triumphantly up at George. "There's one thing you didn't know, third dimensional man. One thing you couldn't know. In the fourth dimension, the female is superior physically."

Arl moaned.

George didn't know a thing about fourth dimensional culture. He had never thought of this possibility, but now Narka held her husband firmly, and she began to do something to his arm.

"Give up?" she said.

Arl looked up at George. "I tried."

"Nuts," said George. "You may think the female is stronger in the fourth dimension, but you're in the third dimension now. If Arl — "

Arl needed that encouragement. He smiled now, and this time his smile was the grim certain one. "Why not?" he said. "Something there — different dimension, different laws apply, and if I can do it once, do it now — "

He writhed fiercely in Narka's grip, and George watched. Someone was knocking at the door. "Open up. Hey, open up in there! I saw you at the window, so I know you're there. What the hell did you throw them pins out for? Open up!"

The knocking became more urgent.

It was important, it was vital. But George hardly heard it. Here at his feet he saw a culture changing. Arl forced his wife slowly up and back, and then Arl was in control. He sat on the floor and Narka was draped across his lap and he was spanking her.

"Remarkable," Myra said.

Narka began to cry. With each downward stroke of Arl's hand, she cried. And by the look on the king's face, George could tell that Arl was having the time of his life.

He didn't want to stop. He was enjoying himself too much, after all these years, and he was in no mood to stop. But George pulled him away. "She's had enough."

Arl was cocky. "Will you be a good girl now, Narka?"

The queen sighed and nodded. She had a look of disbelief on her face, but she walked off into the corner of the room. She looked as if she wanted to sit down, but then she thought better of it, and she stood there, sulking.

"Quick," George said. He helped Arl gather up the jewels, and even Myra helped, and then Narka was telling Arl, listlessly, where she had gotten them. Arl winked at George, his arms loaded with the treasures, and then he disappeared.

GEORGE opened the door. The cop stalked in, belligerently. "Now, what's going on? What's going on in here, that's what I wanna know!"

George frowned. "What do you mean, officer?"

"I mean, these jewels." He held out his hand, showing the three expensive items he had caught. "Better explain this good, bud."

There was only one thing to do, George thought. "Explain it? Explain what? What jewels are you talking about, officer?"

"These damn jewels in my hand, that's what!" The cop held his hand out, showing the two brooches and the necklace.

"I don't see any jewels," said

George. "Myra, do you see any jewels?"

"Huh? Why, of course — not. I don't see anything."

"Narka?"

The queen looked sullen, but she shook her head. "No."

George looked at the policeman. "Tch, tch," he said, shaking his head.

"What do you mean, no jewels? You hinting I'm nuts?"

"Maybe just a few drinks too many," George suggested, looking at the jewelry.

"Why, listen — " But the policeman scratched his head.

He didn't see Arl come up behind him. Arl reached out and grabbed the two brooches, the necklace — and then disappeared.

The policeman looked at his hand. For a long time he stared at it. His jaw went slack.

"Jeez — " he said.

"We'll forget it," George told him. "We'll forget all about it. Now just go home and behave yourself — and no drinking on duty, eh officer?"

"Yeah. Yeah, sure." The cop went out the door, still staring at his hand.

In a moment, Arl was back. Narka looked at him, and George had seen that look in Myra's eyes yesterday at their bungalow. Arl took his wife's arm in a firm grip. "We're going home," he said.

She looked dubious, but then she rubbed her posterior, and she smiled ruefully. "Yes, m'lord." Arl shook hands with George, waved to Myra — and then they disappeared.

George smiled. "Let that be a lesson to you, dear."

Myra kissed him, shyly. They had been married for six years, but it was a shy kiss.

"I don't need any lesson, George."

"No more Fort? No more psychokinesis?"

"No more, if you say so, George."

"I say so."

"Yes, sir," said Myra. "Yes, sir."

THE END

THE VIOLENT ELEMENT

At the moment, Man is Earthbound—and this maddening frustration is inducing engineers and scientists into such a lather of activity that it is perfectly possible that the victory will come sooner than we think. For there is only one reason why we haven't penetrated into space. It's just one simple maddening reason—we don't have the fuel!

Everything else is there. We have the metals and the alloys. We have the navigational and electronic equipment. We have the general know-how of rocketry. But alas, no fuel.

The present combinations of phenol and nitric acid, of alcohol and liquid oxygen, of different organic fuels and liquid oxygen—all of these are good—but not good enough. They'll drive rockets at thousands of miles an hour, but none of them will combine this power with escape velocity so that, for example, a projectile can be launched at the Moon.

These fuels are also good enough for warfare here on Earth. But for Man's ultimate adventure they're not powerful enough. As a result there is a frantic search for things to do the job. Every conceivable line, no matter how dangerous, is being explored. Liquid hydrogen and oxygen are being considered.

Recently scientists have turned toward Nature's most devastating element—liquid fluorine! Of all the compounds and elements known to science this is unquestionably the most terrible. It is a virulent gas at normal temperature which will attack everything—it is the nearest thing to the Universal Solvent which exists. It can only be kept in metal cylinders because of the fact that it immediately attacks them forming a protective coating of one of its fluorides. It is a tremendously powerful oxidizing agent—and, that's it! An answer to rocketry. We need just such a thing.

Fluorine with hydrogen is being contemplated and experimented with. It may provide another step toward the necessary ranges and speeds of the super rockets to come. As it stands now, theoretically fluorine in combination with hydrogen in a rocket motor, offers a chance for a range some two and a half times as great as with any other fuels. The great problem is handling the two virulent violent elements of liquid oxygen and liquid fluorine. Alone they are bad enough; together they are impossible.

But technology never admits of the impossible. It will find some way to handle and control these dreadful chemical agents. We can regard this combination as an intermediate step. It appears as if for a final solution we're going to have to look into some sort of an atomic motor. This is still a long way off though—and we don't want to wait!

Man must get to the Moon. It's so near—it's so within the realm of attainment. Must we be held up for the lack of something so simple? We have a strong suspicion that this condition won't last much longer.

THE OLD ONES

By Betsy Curtis

Illustrated by Ramon Raymond

They had outlived their usefulness on Earth and society waited patiently for them to die. Thus it was only natural for them to seek a new world . . .

DR. Warner didn't usually burst into Dr. Farrar's office. Usually he paced slowly up the hospital corridor, pulling down his glistening white lastijac uniform, meditating on all the mistakes he might have made during the past week, reluctantly turning the knob on the outer door, hesitatingly asking Miss Herrington if the doctor wished to see him now, stepping humbly through the inner door into the presence. But this morning he burst in and slammed the inner door.

"Two this morning in Block Nineteen!" he blurted. "Two suicides at once; Saul Forsythe and Madam LePays!"

Only a few minutes before, Dr. Farrar had been reading and sighing, sighing at the thought that there were no excitements left, only annoyances and minor gratifications.

"The publication of *The One-Hundred-Year-Old in the Culture of Today* marks the date of another notable contribution to human understanding by the justly famous young doctor, Jules Farrar." The review grew more laudatory from paragraph to glowing paragraph. Dr. Farrar, re-reading it word by word, was inclined to smile at the adjective 'young'; he was fifty-eight and felt every day of it this smiling spring morning. He ran his hand back over his head smoothing the place where, twenty years ago, there had been hair. He looked up from the paper on his desk, through the glimmering sunlight at the row of dark green file cases banking the opposite end of the office, the first five now ticketed "closed" and the "closed" sign lying on top of the sixth, the 100-year case. He gazed on down the row—110, 120, 130, 140 and the rest—and sighed deeply. Futility washed over him, and an echo of the old story of the man who wrote his autobiography taking a year to write the doings of each day. The job would never be finished and the amusement of writing of youth was too far behind.

He quoted grimly from his own *Sixty-Year-Old*, "Among males at this time, the conviction, often amounting to panic, that the time for accomplishment is almost past begins to grow and obscure the comfortable mellowness of being in the midst of important activity." How could he have known so much at thirty and still have arrived at almost sixty without having solved anything, discovered anything new, done nothing but descriptive studies steadily for thirty-five years? And there were no excitements left —nothing but annoyances.

His office door now flew open with a crash against the 50-year file case, then was banged shut again and Bob Warner's white-jacketed body was leaning toward him over his desk.

"Two suicides at once, Dr. Farrar!" Dr. Warner was almost shouting at him, "and one last week and four others in the past year! They'll investigate us and upset the subjects and everybody. They'll get out of Block Nineteen and go poking around in genetics and new diseases and want to know where and why every cent is being spent and wind up trying to cut the staff or change the diets or some other stupidity." (Jules Farrar smiled wryly: there had been two Congressional investigations at the hospital since he came, and Bob's description from hearsay was all too accurate.) "I tell you, Doctor, we've got to hush this up. Congress won't let us get away with firing a couple of floor nurses this time!" Ione Phillips was in Nineteen and much too pretty for a scapegoat. It wasn't his responsibility anyway. "What are we going to do, Doctor?"

"Saul Forsythe and Madame LePays," Jules Farrar's voice was low with concern, "How old were they? What was the matter?"

"Madame was 182 and Forsythe was a year or two older. There wasn't anything wrong that I know. They'd both been reading last night. He had the last volume of the *Britannica* and she had a little old book of poems—French poems."

"No animosities, no quarrels with other subjects?"

"No, no! They weren't very social types, you know; we haven't had much culture-pattern data on either of them for some time. It's not as if they were a great loss to the experiments," he added reassuringly. Mustn't get old Farrar upset.

THE older doctor looked oddly at the younger. "There must be something wrong in Block Nineteen. We'll call a meeting of staff. You can't cover up this sort of thing, Doctor. Everybody probably knows it already. You know how nurses gossip. But we'd better talk to Daneshaw first. He's always sound on what's going on in Block Nineteen."

"But Dr. Farrar, Daneshaw can't bring them back. He's just another subject. You could swear the nurses to secrecy for the good of the hospital. It's not as if it were anything strange or exciting. If we get an investigation, the subjects will run amok. Blood pressures will go up and some of them won't eat and others won't sleep thinking up fancy stories to tell the investigating commission and the smooth curve charts will be all shot to . . . "

Farrar laughed, "Intriguing thought, a thousand near-200-year-oldsters running amok. But seriously, if they kill themselves off this way, it will mess things up. Don't worry about your job yet, Doctor. Daneshaw will think of something. On your way out, ask Miss Herrington to get in touch with him. Now you get back to Block Nineteen and see that everything stays quiet for a while. I'd rather not have an investigation either."

"But, Doctor . . . "

"It's an order. Well, on second thought, get everybody over 150 out of the hospital on an expedition of some kind." He scribbled on a pad.

"But, Dr. Farrar . . . "

"Here's an order for cars . . . and . . . (writing) . . . buses and field kitchens. Take them out in the country for a picnic. Come back here as soon as you can get away." He held out a paper.

"A picnic! For a thousand?"

"You can do it. You're the best organizer in the hospital."

"Well . . . I suppose so."

"Excellent," concluded Dr. Farrar and rose, indicating dismissal.

"Daneshaw will think of something," he repeated to himself as Warner walked out and slammed the door.

R. N. Ione Phillips flounced down Corridor Five of Block Nineteen, white elaston uniform rustling with permanent and indignant starch.

"Those old biddies," she muttered. "Both of them say they want lilac pattern dresses and then when they come they're mad because they have dresses just alike. They're just like children!" Miss Phillips didn't care much for children.

"Won't wash for meals but spend hours taking up all the driers in the beauty salon. Bob Warner doesn't realize what we have to put up with."

Her angry stalk slowed to a demure mincing as she approached the elevator and imagined Dr. Warner coming out of it.

Behind the door she had just closed with apparently thoughtful gentleness, Mrs. Maeva McGaughey and Mrs. Alice Kaplan in lilac acelle were considering the meal on the table between them.

"Creamed spinach, Maeva, for breakfast!" Mrs. Kaplan was withering in her distaste.

"And that Miss Phillips—treats us as if we were babies," whined Mrs. McGaughey. "The way she talks you'd think she'd brought us a couple of wedding gowns. Shoddy stuff these days, too."

Mrs. Kaplan looked slyly at Mrs. McGaughey. "I know how to fix her, Maeva. Let's pour this spinach down our fronts."

IONE had reached the end of the corridor and was tripping abstractedly by the desk facing the row of elevators.

"Phillips," the receptionist's voice was startling and cool, "will you tell Mr. Daneshaw, Room 563, that Dr. Farrar would like to see him at once in his office."

"It's my breakfast hour! I'm just going off duty." Receptionists thought they owned the hospital ordering people around all the time.

"I can't leave the desk and your relief hasn't come up. Dr. Farrar says it's urgent."

"Oh, all right." Ione turned on her heel and strode with something of the old swish up the hall to the left of the one she'd come from.

She knocked sharply at the door of room 563. "Mr. Daneshaw?"

"Come in."

She turned the knob and economically stuck only her head around the frame. "Dr. Farrar wants you in his office at once." She withdrew and closed the door in one motion. Don't give them a chance to argue or ask questions. They'd waste your whole day for you if you gave them a chance. She headed for the elevators once more.

Professor Emeritus Charles Timothy Daneshaw had lain in bed in the comfortable insulation of the bulky grey plastine autometab case which covered him to the waist. He really enjoyed this five minutes after waking when the world was entirely shut off and he could collect his thoughts for the day with no other business but regular inhale and exhale.

Sweet day, so calm, so cool, so bright, he quoted mentally. This was a comfortable poem for springtime in one's 186th year. *The bridal of the earth and sky, The dews shall weep thy fall tonight, For thou must die.* No one would have to weep for him. He wasn't going to die. He would walk on the lawns today and enjoy the burgeoning of spring without pain, without fear. He would read Wordsworth and plan a vacation walking trip.

The bell next to his ear pinged—the machine had finished his daily metabolic record—he pressed the button that raised the heavy case to the ceiling. He stretched and put his feet over the edge of the bed.

Sweet spring, full of sweet days and roses, he headed for the bathroom, *A box where sweets compacted lie.* The shaving cabinet was not such a box. He had to stoop to see the shock of white hair in the mirror, and shaving was a daily nuisance in a bent-kneed position. Some architect must have decided that it was the custom for old men not to be over five feet eight and installed accordingly. Old men should be bowed down with years, but Tim Daneshaw was still six feet three in spite of four inches shrinkage since his thirties, his tall body still unbowed by years or habit.

Only a sweet and virtuous soul, like seasoned timber never gives . . . he was finishing the Herbert quotation as he wiped off the remaining shaving soap, when there was a sharp rap on the outer door of his room.

"Mr. Daneshaw?"

"Come in."

"Dr. Farrar wants you in his office at once." Miss Phillips' white-capped head bobbed in and out, the door shut, and he could hear the click of her retreating heels.

He stepped out of the bathroom and began pulling on his clothes. "Poor Jules," he mused. "Hard at work on a beautiful spring morning before I've even had breakfast. Maybe he'll give me a cup of coffee."

HE was halfway to the elevator, pacing slowly, imagining the aroma of a hot cup of coffee, seeing a thin twist of steam, when a door opened a few steps ahead of him. A wiry little man in a maroon bathrobe beckoned.

"Come in here a minute, Tim," said the little man, his voice almost a whisper.

"Jules wants me over in Administration Block, El."

Elbert Avery grabbed Daneshaw's arm. "He can wait. This is important, Tim."

"Just for a minute, then. The nurse said 'at once'." He went in and Avery closed the door quickly.

"Have you heard about Saul and Clarice? How they both got out this morning?" Avery seated himself in the swivel chair beside the tremendous desk that made his room look much smaller than Daneshaw's.

"Got out?"

"They were both found dead this morning at breakfast time. I just heard about it. Saul cut his wrist with his razor and Clarice fiddled with the autometab so it wouldn't raise and then went to sleep in it. Some people are just born with more nerve than others!" Avery sounded actually envious.

"This is no joke, El." Tim Daneshaw leaned against the high white bed. "Don't talk that way to anybody—there's nothing noble in killing yourself and you know you wouldn't do it even if you had the chance."

"Oh, I don't know," responded the little man defiantly, tipping back in his chair. "What's the percentage in living on here forever? Nobody knows what you were and nobody cares what you are and there's not one damn thing worth spending ten minutes on that they don't say, 'Take it easy, don't strain yourself, don't get worked up, why don't you take a rest or play a nice relaxing game of checkers.' I don't like pet mice and I think raffia baskets are an abomination. You're right about suicide not being noble —it's just common sense!"

"Elbert, Elbert," Tim was gentle, reproachful, "wait a minute. Everybody here knows how you built up Avery, Inc. singlehanded into the biggest transport corporation in the world and how you bowed out to let younger men have their chance at running the most successful business in the country." He came over and perched on the edge of the desk close to Avery. "You know the Block Nineteen Association wouldn't even be able to buy Christmas cards if you weren't handling our little investments. There isn't one person on this experiment that doesn't respect you."

"On this experiment, hell!" exploded Avery. "There isn't anybody in Block Nineteen that doesn't know I ran out when the government began hemming in big corporations with thousands of petty restrictions on mansized business so that a company president was nothing more than a yes-man to a regiment of lawyers and government accountants. If the boys in Washington knew I was handling a little stock for Block Nineteen they'd think of some way to close us up in five minutes. They'd be just as happy if they knew I was out of the way."

"But you are a genius at keeping your tracks covered and we do need you. We'll need you especially at the block meeting today," soothed

Daneshaw.

"The meeting's not till day after tomorrow," Avery objected.

"We'll have to hold it now before some of us forget we're grown up and start going to pieces like the two this morning you were so excited about a minute ago." He paused. "I just can't understand it about Clarice LePays. She was so self-possessed, a charming and dignified woman. We will miss her, Elbert. She added a great deal of grace to our gatherings."

"Grace! She was just another old woman in a young woman's world. Don't be a hypocrite, Tim."

Daneshaw got up. "Anyhow, you have a job now. It's up to you and me as officers of the Block Nineteen Association to keep the others calm and give them something else to think about. You put that magic brain of yours to work on that while I go down to see Jules. I'll tell him we must have our meeting today." He put his hand on the knob.

"Calm, bah!" Avery bit the end off a stogy and spat it at the floor vehemently. "You better warn that Jules Farrar that his guinea pigs are sick and tired of his hotel-concentration-camp and of the whole world where we don't belong. I hope he lives to be a million."

"I'll tell him what you say," smiled Daneshaw grimly. "Now you get to work on a speech." He went out, a set smile still on his face.

WHEN the amber light showed on the intercom on his desk, Dr. Farrar flipped the switch and barked a brief, "Send him in!"

Expecting the lanky white-maned Daneshaw in familiar heather-tweed, he was shocked by the appearance of the natty little man in midnight-blue dulfin slacks and ultra-conservative tabarjak. A Congressman so soon? He rose, extended his hand, half expecting the newcomer to refuse it coldly.

This little man smiled and grasped the outstretched hand heartily, saying, "Dr. Farrar? I'm Jeremy Brill of Far-Western Insurance and Annuity. Your secretary said you might have some time to spare this morning." He relinquished the hand and Dr. Farrar was freed to motion him to the green easy chair at the right of the desk.

"Glad to know you." He wasn't—he was lining up a few words for Miss Herrington on the subject of admitting salesmen. "Miss Herrington was mistaken, though, about my having much time. Something important has come up in the hospital this morning. Another day might be much better if you have anything extensive to discuss." He tried to remain courteous, keep his voice pleasant.

"I won't take but a few minutes of your day, Dr. Farrar, but there is a matter upon which The Company needs advice from you as soon as possible."

This sounded different from the usual opening. "Yes? What can I do for you?"

"You have a large group of patients here, Doctor, all of whom are well over a hundred years old."

"Not patients, Mr. Brill. Subjects. Subjects for observation on patterns of old age."

"Subjects, then. Well, a considerable number of these subjects have annuities with us and it is of great concern to us to have some estimate of their present condition."

"You mean physiologically? This group is in excellent health."

"Not exactly," the little man leaned forward confidentially. "We are more concerned with their mental state. You probably know that when a person is adjudged mentally incompetent or even gravely 'insecure,' the state takes over the care and support of such a person and The Company is released from financial obligation to that person. As a tremendous taxpayer, The Company aids in state support, but not to the extent of, shall we say, a perpetual annuity."

"Oh, I see. The company is feeling the pinch of a few long-term payments to those subjects of ours and would like to have them put away to cut expenses?" Dr. Farrar could not completely keep the scorn out of his voice.

"Oh, no, Doctor. You misunderstand me completely." Brill's tones were rich with wounded innocence. "The Company only wants to know what are the probabilities of mental breakdown at different ages, say a hundred and sixty, a hundred and eighty, two hundred. If we had some assurance of even a slight but definite tendency to, shall we say, mental erosion, with an increase in age above a hundred and fifty, The Company might find it possible to continue some such annuity plan as is now in operation." The man talked like an annual report, it seemed to Dr. Farrar, but with the difference that it had something to do with him.

"You or your medical colleagues," Brill went on brightly, "have done humanity yeoman service. Not only have you lengthened life and made living it less painful, but you have reduced the consumer-costs of life insurance to a level which makes premiums ridiculously low. Of course," he added complacently, "this has resulted in a great increase in the number of the insured and the size and scope of The Company."

"But if people are going to live forever, your company is going to have to discontinue the annuity system, is that it?" Dr. Farrar asked pointedly. "You'd leave the old folks cut off from jobs by custom and from any other income by expediency?"

JEREMY Brill was suddenly serious. "The problem of the support of paupers is hardly the immediate responsibility of Far-Western. Besides," he added hopefully, "by the time the thirty-year olders whose policies we would have to refuse to write now are old enough to worry about it, our society will no doubt have found some way for them to maintain their independence. I have the greatest faith in you social researchers, so great that my company can surely feel free to turn that problem over to you with utter confidence.

"And perhaps, as a matter of fact," he continued, "you can already tell me that there is little hope that man can pass his two-hundredth year without serious impairment of his faculties, and we shall only have to raise the age at which annuities begin to pay. The Company naturally prefers the gentle road of reform to the cataclysm of revolution." He relaxed after this burst of metaphor.

"I am not at all sure that there is any sanity data on those over 150 in statistical form. It would take me some time to be sure of any exact present correlation of mental erosion, as you call it, with age." Dr. Farrar reflected on the state of the file cases in the further corner. He wasn't at all sure, either, how much it was wise to tell this eager representative of The Company. (Mr. Brill always said it as if "The Company" were written entirely in capital letters.) There might be other angles. This increase in suicide, for instance.

"You see," he went on, "Block Nineteen does not have a very high complement of psychiatrists. If the subjects get too difficult to handle, we usually send them to Mayhew Mental Observing Hospital and close their files here. We do chiefly physiological research here, you know. The older subjects seem to mistrust young psychiatrists and the more practical men seem to prefer working in places like the Mayhew where the material is more interesting." Maybe he could get rid of the man by offering a better bait.

"The Company would be more than willing to offer the services of a couple of trained statistical analysts if you would like to put your unorganized material at our disposal for, shall we say, a week?"

So that was the angle—let The Company in on the files where they would uncover a number of other interesting things—the suicides too, as the other subjects reacted to them. Now he'd have to take time off, at work on the *Hundred-and-Ten-Year-Old* to dig about in the advanced data. One couldn't violate the privacy of the records, not at this moment, anyhow.

"That won't be necessary, thanks. I could have some word for you in a couple of weeks—as soon as certain other matters are taken care of. I'd be interested in the results myself, naturally." And he would.

There might be some clue to poor Clarice LePays and Forsythe and the earlier ones. A promise of figures soon would put Brill off temporarily. Now change the subject and close the talk.

"I suppose you have to do a lot of odd investigating like this in the course of company work?" Dr. Farrar asked politely.

"Yes, indeed, Doctor. Every event in the world is somehow connected with the insurance business. You might be interested to know that some of our men are now in Washington investigating space ship conditions. Confidentially, we shall probably soon be pushing a government subsidy for insurance for space crews and extra-territorial colonists. Sounds fantastic, doesn't it?"

"I should say so. But I thought the *Colonia* wasn't due to take off for another year. I rather lose track of world news in my job here."

"She'd be ready to blast in fourteen months if they could decide about passengers and crew. Every nation in the Assembly and every bloc from farm and free-lifers to commists wants to be the first to start the colony, mostly from distrust of the others, but no particular individuals seem to want to be the first to cut the ties. The crew has to stay with the colony for months, you know, until they're settled and know what else they need. The *Colonia's* the only large ship under construction. The Company doesn't want to be responsible for possible mishaps and we've just started writing in space-travel exception clauses in our regular policies."

THE intercom bulb burned amber again. This time Farrar was more cautious.

"Who is it?" he asked.

"Mr. Daneshaw."

"Send him in in about a minute."

He turned to Brill. "The man who's coming in is one of our older subjects. You might like to meet him." He smiled. "Not that he's exactly typical of his age."

"You won't tell him why I'm here?" Brill requested. "The Company naturally doesn't want any publicity on this matter, yet Doctor."

"Naturally, Mr. Brill, you don't want a run on annuity policies any more than the Government wants to alarm prospective settlers on Venus by refusing to insure them. Old Daneshaw has probably forgotten more secrets than we'll ever know: but if you think best . . . "

"I do."

The door swung back smoothly, stopping just short of the file cases, to admit the tall tweed-clad figure of the professor emeritus, who closed it gently, deliberately.

"Morning, Tim."

"Good morning, Jules." Daneshaw noticed the stranger and stood uncertaintly just inside the door.

"I'd like to introduce Mr. Brill —Mr. Daneshaw."

Daneshaw's handshake was firm but gentle like his closing of the door. He moved to the maple armchair and sat, crossing his long legs, relaxed.

"Mr. Brill's got a great-aunt on the waiting list for Block Nineteen. He's here looking us over to see if we're fit company."

Mr. Daneshaw looked a question at the doctor, who continued, "Mr. Brill is in the insurance business. He's been telling me about one of their recent problems—whether or not to insure space crews and extraterrestrial colonists. On the *Colonia,* you know."

Daneshaw roused suddenly and turned an eager face to Brill. "That's a great thing! Never thought I'd see the day, though I was quite a science-fiction fan in my eighties and nineties. I've read everything I could lay my hands on about the *Colonia*. Do you really know who the colonists are going to be—or is that a secret between the United Assembly and the insurance companies?"

Brill looked pleased. This nice old boy realized the confidence of The Powers in The Company. "It hasn't been settled yet—may take months more the way they're wrangling. The Chinese don't want it to be the Dutch and the Dutch don't want the Brazilians. You know how it is. Myself, I think the government bit off more than it could chew, offering the first American built ship to whatever group the Assembly decided to send."

DR. Farrar winced inwardly. A political discussion with Tim Daneshaw would certainly antagonize Brill if not exhaust him. "Who would you like to see go, Tim?" he veered the talk away from the errors of the present regime.

"I suppose farmers would be the first choice—big scale men with experience in hydroponics, from what I know of conditions on Venus."

"But the Assembly seems to be set against any group now economically favored," Brill offered the objection condescendingly, "and small farmers as a class have some sort of prejudice against any type of farming or scenery except what they grew up with."

"Well, speaking purely academically, Mr. Brill, I think the Assembly could do worse than send us."

"Us?"

"Us old duffers. Economically speaking, we're nobodies, our local ties are the weakest, we are of no particular value to anybody except Dr. Farrar here," he waved a hand, "and we're obviously of no political danger to the Chinese or the commists or the insulars either. We're not even a bloc. But of course we wouldn't please anybody especially as colonists, either. It's only an academic suggestion, you understand."

He grinned first at Brill, and at Farrar. "We couldn't put the good Jules out of a job, of course."

The intercom light flashed at the same moment that the door was flung open. Dr. Warner was halfway to the desk before he noticed the other visitors. He stopped abruptly.

"What is it, Doctor?" Dr. Farrar's voice was mildly reproachful. "Do you need me?"

"Excuse me, Doctor. The fleet is ready for the picnic and I thought you might have some last minute . . . that is . . . I didn't know what plans . . . " Dr. Warner mumbled, confused at finding a stranger in the office.

"This is Mr. Brill—Dr. Warner. Doctor, Mr. Brill's great-aunt is on our waiting list for Block Nineteen and he is concerned with our program and facilities here. Do you suppose you could take him with you on the picnic this morning?"

Jeremy Brill was startled. "I don't want to be any trouble, Doctor," he said apologetically to both doctors at once.

"No trouble at all, Mr. Brill," reassured Dr. Farrar. "You go with Dr. Warner here. He'll find a place in one of the limousines and you'll have a chance to talk to lots of the people your aunt would have to live with—make some judgment for yourself about all the items we were discussing. You can have Mr. Daneshaw's lunch on the picnic. He's staying here with me today."

Brill bowed his thanks to Daneshaw and Dr. Farrar and rose.

Jules Farrar turned to Dr. Warner. "Give them a good time, Bob. There aren't any special plans, but if you should happen to pass a circus, take the whole gang. Do you have plenty of money? This is on the hospital."

If Bob Warner had been alone with his chief he would have shouted, "A circus—ye gods!" but with Brill and Daneshaw both present he didn't even dare splutter. He nodded mechanically for Brill to precede him out the office door. Just before closing it after them, he stuck his head back into the office and enunciated with great care, "Thank you for the lovely treat, Doctor!" and was gone.

THERE was silence in the office for a few moments after the two had left.

Both men spoke at once. "Tim, have you heard . . . " "Two deaths, Jules."

Both were silent again. Neither looked at the other.

Dr. Farrar started again. "Why did it happen, Tim? What's the trouble up there? What have we done or not done?"

"They were bored and lonely and useless. Nothing you could have done, I'm afraid. Others feel the same way. There will have to be some smart talking at an Association meeting tonight to make them forget it."

Dr. Farrar looked keenly at the old man. "You too, Tim? Do you want to join Forsythe and Madame?

Daneshaw looked straight at the doctor. "No, not me, That's why it will be hard for me to talk to them. I've been enjoying myself the whole time—sitting back, waiting and watching to see how our problems were going to be solved, indulging my curiosity about things, looking on with a rather Jovian amusement and tolerance to see how the young ones would have to learn how to deal with the old ones when they found out how many of us there were going to be. I thought I had all the time in the world to wait, so I've just been taking it easy and having quite a good time. It's really more my fault than yours."

"It's not your fault, Tim; I suppose it's mine. I thought that my studies would lose their validity if I stepped in and changed factors in your way of living. I totally ignored the changes involved in bringing you all here out of a normal life pattern with nothing but little diddling make-work substitutes to keep you busy."

"What would you call normal for us? We didn't even diddle before we came here."

"I should have remembered, though. I did a lot of work on the 'suicide period' between 60 and 70 seventeen years ago. There were only a couple hundred of the present Block Nineteener's and new ones coming all the time to keep things stirred up and interesting. I got so used to having things change up there every day that I never noticed when it began to bog down. It was my problem, Tim, and I ignored it."

"Ours, too, Jules. We ought to be responsible adults by now, capable of working out our own troubles." Daneshaw uncrossed his legs and sat forward. "But we aren't going to get anywhere sitting here worrying about which of us is to blame. We've got to cook up something more important than another kind of pet to keep or another bridge tournament. Wordsworth was evidently wrong. He should have written '*Not* getting and *not* spending we lay waste our powers.' We ought to be up to the ears in the work of a lifetime . . . a very long lifetime." His lean hand brushed back unruly white locks.

Dr. Farrar shrugged his shoulders. "Any suggestions?"

"Whatever it is," argued Daneshaw, "it ought to be as important as . . . as the *Colonia* trip to Venus. It's certainly as vital as that, though of course having the Federal Government of the United Assembly messing with the problem would put off a solution indefinitely."

A look of wonder grew on the doctor's face. "The *Colonia!* A colony! How about that? The hospital has funds. We could buy a piece of land somewhere in the wilds of Brazil or even Canada and you could have a shot at frontier problems. That ought to be absorbing enough. And of course you could have help from government experts here if you ran into trouble. How about it?" he asked eagerly.

"It smacks of the county poor farm, though the idea of a colony is rather appealing. I hate to be a wet blanket, but the prospect of government experts seems like a continuation of the kindly but firm handling we get from the nurses here," and Tim Daneshaw smiled ruefully remembering Ione Phillips and how well she "handled" the subjects. "I'm afraid that unless we could get as far away from supervision as Venus we'd go right on feeling like a second thumb."

"Then go to Venus! On the first ship out." Jules sobered suddenly. "It would take an ungodly amount of finagling . . . do you think they'd really go?"

"It would be worth asking them tonight." (There was no harm in joining in a flight of imagination, when a real solution might take years.) "And you know, we could be more of a nuisance to the government than you could ever be. We could threaten to commit suicide *en masse* and blackmail the government into backing us for fear of one of those social breakdown investigations by the United Assembly, and we could fix the Assembly by threatening to flood the international publications with articles about the mental horrors of old age and break down the whole socialized medicine convention at the international level. It might be rather fun . . . though completely unethical."

The doctor got up and came around to sit on the front of the desk. He was beaming. "Tim, we'll try it. I think I can get help from Brill. I'll tell you about it later. We've got to get right to work, though."

"We?"

"I can't pull it off alone," he paused, staring intently into Daneshaw's face. "I want you to go to the U. A. headquarters . . . right now. Parker can take you to Des Moines in my copter and you'll get a rocket there. Miss Herrington will make your reservation. I want you to get all the stuff you can on number of passengers, agricultural projects, known difficulties of settlement on Venus—everything about the *Colonia.* And especially how to go about making application for the first group of colonists. I'll call Spence, the ranking medical officer of the U. A. We were friends in school. He can meet you and find out in advance who you should see. On the way you can work up something to tell the meeting tonight." Dr. Farrar seemed to see the plan growing in the air in front of him.

"That's quite an order for an old man—but it should be fun. What shall I tell the people I have to see why I want to know all this?"

"Tell them it's a secret . . . Social Medical priority A four-ones. That'll get 'em interested and if they can find out somehow what it's all about by private investigation they'll be more likely to back us because they'll be in on what they think is top-secret."

"Smart, aren't you Jules." Tim got up and grasped his hand. "It'll be quite thrilling while it lasts. I feel pretty selfish, having all the fun to myself." He turned and strode to the door. "I'll go up and get a hat while the .copter is coming—guess I don't even need a toothbrush."

"Tim," Dr. Farrar was hesitant, "do you have a pin-stripe tabarjak . . . or anything like that?"

"Diplomat duds, you mean?" grinned the departing Daneshaw. "I've got a full set for Princeton reunions. I'll knock their eyes out."

IT was hardly half past two when Jeremy Brill returned to the hospital. Dr. Farrar, returning from a belated lunch, found him fidgeting in the waiting room, making notes on a pocket pad. He rose quickly and followed the doctor into the inner office, carefully closing the door.

"I've heard enough, Doctor," he blurted out as he reached for the straight chair near the desk. "Enough to last a long time. They're sane, but what sanity! That Avery!"

"Have a little talk with Avery, did you?" inquired Dr. Farrar. He thought the two of them must have been well matched.

"First I heard all about the business of 'relax and save your energy forever'."

The doctor smiled. "Standard indoctrination for longevity subjects."

"Then he asked what I did. I told him a little about our work in The Company and that set him off! The man's a menace. He knows more about The Company than I do." Brill's suavity was quite gone. "And what a rugged tyrant he must have been. Positively treasonable in his attacks on governmental regulation. He believes in business for the businessman—thinks only people with capacity for handling high finance ought to run the country for the country's good. It was heresy —appalling!"

"I was rather of the opinion," commented the doctor, "that the views of your company ran something along the same line."

"Not at all, *not at all!* We believe firmly in the committee system and systematic regulation by elected agencies. There can be no grand-scale despotism in The Company! Why, our officers receive psychotesting every six months to assure the policy-holders that they have no personal power ambitions. I tell you, Doctor, that such men as Elbert Avery are a threat to our national democracy. He seems perfectly capable of going back into business at the drop of a hat. The Company may have to send a man to Washington to work out some sort of control to prevent such men from re-entering business."

Dr. Farrar looked thoughtful. "The control would be easy enough, but expensive," he remarked doubtfully.

"The good of the country is always expensive."

"What would you think of sending this whole group of social misfits out of the country?" Dr. Farrar could be cagy.

"Force, Doctor? We couldn't do that."

"But you'd like to see 'em go?"

"Frankly, yes."

"And if the government would take over the annuities, you'd feel even better?"

"That is too much for The Company to ask." Brill was resigned now, almost wistful.

Dr. Farrar settled himself back in his chair. "I have a plan, Mr. Brill; and perhaps you might be able to help me." (Brill sat forward.) "I would like to see Block Nineteen emptied completely — I would like to see its present occupants migrate to Venus on the *Colonia*. I don't think they'd ever come back. That would give your company several years to work out its new policy scheme and would remove what you call a dangerous menace to a safe distance. The next generation of Old Ones will be better schooled in ridding themselves of 'personal power ambition.' Do you think it could be done?"

"Perhaps," Brill was slow to hope. "The Company certainly has the organization to put it through. But you'd never get them to go. Why, Avery thinks the whole *Colonia* enterprise is financially unsound. He says it's the duty of every thinking man to do all he can to stop such ruinous nonsense. Colonization *is* expensive, but it is undoubtedly best for the people of the world! . . . But that old Avery doesn't give a hang for the Assembly's making a gift of Venus to the people."

"Avery would go like a shot rather than be left behind. And he's only one out of a thousand. You'd be willing to help?"

BRILL hitched his chair even closer to the desk. "Just tell me first why you are so anxious to get rid of your entire observational group? Naturally The Company doesn't want to get mixed up in any personal animosities or anything unethical. Why do *you* want to get rid of them, Doctor?"

"If I can trust you to keep this as quiet as your company's interest in moving them out?"

"Yes."

"To be quite frank, then, the subjects in Block Nineteen are getting restless. I don't think we could keep them here more than ten years longer, no matter how many diversions we tried. They want to do something, be something. And yet I don't believe they could be any more miserable than back in a world which has been growing away from them for a hundred years, a world which doesn't want or understand them any more than you want Avery in your company. So I'd naturally rather see them go all at once, wanting to go, than one at a time, confused and hopeless. None of them want to go back to their great-great-grandchildren to die. I'd like to see them stay together. As for my research, I'm only up to the Hundred-and-Ten group. Those in Block Nineteen are all over a hundred and fifty. Do you want to help . . . or would you rather go to Washington to lobby for a bill to control Avery and others with even more ancient ideas before they get loose?"

"But old people are set in their ways, as you know, Doctor." Jeremy Brill had memorized the salesman's book. "The Company would naturally have to have some assurance that the old ones are willing to go before we put a lot of time and money into pushing their acceptance as colonists."

"I can let you know by midnight tonight," Dr. Farrar stated positively. "They're holding their monthly meeting and I can see that the matter is given full consideration."

Somewhere inside Dr. Farrar, the conspiratorial feeling was joined by a great jubiliation. He wanted to shout aloud, but instead he added, "The officers of The Company will naturally want time to consider this fully, with care and deliberation. It is fortunate that you will have a good many hours in which to prepare a sound and compelling statement about the benefit to all humanity which will accrue to a project which will settle at once the great problem of a goal for old age as well as end the bitter wrangling among national and political groups for first passage on the *Colonia.*

"You are right. I must get back to the home office at once." Brill scribbled on a card. "Here is my private phone. Let me know at once what is decided at the meeting."

He rose, extending his hand. "You are a great man, Doctor, a truly great and kind man." He wheeled and walked abruptly from the office, the weight of a noble enterprise sitting comfortably on his shoulders. Miss Herrington caught a few of his departing words and the admiring tone, "One stone . . . so many birds."

JULES Farrar's call to Jeremy Brill at 10:57 that night was necessarily brief. Mr. Daneshaw told him nothing of the wrangle with Avery and several others about the inevitable failure of any scheme so economically unsound as extraterrestrial colonization, nor did he tell the doctor that the number who wanted to go for the sake of going was considerably smaller than the number of those who would do anything that he, Tim Daneshaw, urged them to do. He reported only two things from the meeting: first, that they were willing to go on one condition; second, that the condition was that they were to be taught to man the *Colonia* and that no younger "snippets" of officers, crew, and particularly medical and nursing staff should go along to hamper them. That was Avery's one victory.

In the three hours' talk about Daneshaw's trip to U. A. headquarters that followed the phone call, the excited doctor almost forgot to ask how the Block Association had taken the morning's deaths.

The old professor ran his hand through his white mane. "You know, Jules, I told them we'd discuss it after the other business and they never got around to it. Even if the trip doesn't come off, the crisis has been smoothed over for now. It's really rather shocking, isn't it?"

And yet, finally, incredibly, the trip really was to "come off." No one man knew more than a fraction of the details, though Jeremy Brill and his beloved Company turned out to be more of a force than even Dr. Farrar visioned in his most facetious dreams.

The doctor did have to be present at the U. A. loyalty tests, however, and would remember the rocking yet silent mirth of the entire commission to his dying day. The old people had been so outspoken, so set in their ways, but what a multitude of ways, that no bloc could be very seriously offended with them as a group. When little old Miss Severinghouse stated firmly, "I can't say as I trust anybody particularly, but President Wilson was a fine man," open-armed affectionate acceptance was assured. Laughter freshened the air; world tensions eased.

THE months that followed were packed with unusual activity. Dr. Farrar, still at the helm of the Riston Physiological Observing Hospital, saw and heard little of it, beyond what he inferred from the questions of the newsporters who were constantly trying to get beyond his office into the guarded privacy of Block Nineteen. He knew what assignments had been given to which of the "post-adults" (a newspaper phrase which had become universal). He knew, for instance, that Tim Daneshaw was at Annapolis with a number of others receiving advanced officer-training to prepare him for command. But he knew no details. He did not know how . . .

. . . Dr. Francis Keighly registered under an alias for a refresher course in the hospital that had borne his name for thirty-odd years. He smilingly declined special work in obstetrics and put down his name for epidemiology, parisitology and degenerative diseases as well as the usual surgery and internal medicine . . .

. . . Thorsten Veere, the pilot of the first moon-rocket, and Arthur Fisher, the designer of the *Colonia,* entered a formal objection to the United Assembly that the slower reflexes of the "post-adults" would make safe landing on Venus an improbability. They were told that they had exactly eleven months and three days to design and install a safe-and-sane mechanical-plus-radar landing device . . .

. . . Maeva McGaughey titrated deftly, dipping the straw-tinted flask behind the mask of the colorimeter and back with smiling approval. The old skill that had made her a master beautician was returning rapidly as she became a Pharmacist's Mate. She hummed softly, abstractedly, unaware of the absence of Miss Phillips' brisk voice saying, "Please stop that buzzing, Mrs. McGaughey. I'm sure I don't know how you expect the other ladies to get any rest with that noise going on . . .'"

. . . Alice Kaplan was having two new dentures made at the clinic. The flourine shortage in Stowe reservoir had not been known when she was a girl and the town had been too small for a dentist of its own. These would be good teeth with which to eat her own cooking. She had already helped the dietician of the hospital work out a more tasty substitute for the eternal creamed spinach for breakfast, though it was rather hampering to try to work up interesting meals with no carbohydrates and practically no animal fats. But she would use these new teeth on good beef-flour muffins and sharp cheese . . .

. . . Ole Sorensen put down the peck measure of mixed concentrates and began to toss forkfuls of fragrant alfalfa hay into the racks before the prize hospital herd. The muscles of his back and shoulders rippled as the fork swung and he moved rapidly down the line of gleaming white mangers. Between the windows behind him hung the placard filched from the Block Nineteen lobby, HASTE WASTES LIFE. Beneath this profound message was scrawled in black crayon, "Life without haste may be waste." . . .

. . . Joe Kolensky, second astrogator of the *Per Aspera,* whistled admiringly over the pages of calculations on the desk before him. That old gheez Avery had come up with another shortcut in Advanced Orbit Plotting. It was a legitimate shortcut, all right, but Joe had only come across it himself after two years of course work. Avery was almost twice as quick as that old Mr. White who used to teach math at Dayton Tech.

"Say, Bill," Joe raised his gaze from the paper and turned to his office-mate who was also checking classwork, "you know what Avery said today? When I tried to compliment him on yesterday's quadrangulations he glowered as if I'd insulted him and said, 'Young man, I was managing billions before jets were invented. Get on with orbits.' What a character . . . "

. . . Elbert Avery worked feverishly over the pile of papers before him. Today's lesson had included a few facts necessary for his calculations. To make room for new pages, he shoved aside Harling and Bame's *Astrogation Handbook*. "Matches for irresponsible brats to play with," he sneered at the book, "and the sooner they get their tootsies burned the sooner they'll learn to leave this stuff alone." He clenched a fist. "Damned if they're going to bankrupt one planet they can't run to settle another one they don't need." He picked up a stilo and plunged back into the determination of the exact point on the course, the precise moment after turnover, at which, with the slightest increase in deceleration he could send the *Colonia* streaking irrevocably into the sun . . .

THE Quarter-Way Party, three months and four days out in space, was an unqualified failure, according to Arnold Forsberg, the *Colonia's* recreation director. Closeted with Captain Daneshaw in the conference room the following evening, he confessed, "Only about eighty people showed at all. They wouldn't dance, they wouldn't sing; only about three tables of bridge and one of eincheesistein, and those were the champions who play every day anyhow. They wouldn't even eat—just picked at the special non-diet refreshments we thought would be such a hit. Most of them didn't bother to dress formally. They just wandered around. Honestly Tim, with ten more months to go I don't know what we're going to do."

"Maybe they have other things on their minds," Tim placated. "First Night Out Party was as gay as they come. A lot of the women have been studying pretty hard, you know; and we've all been conditioned to taking things calmly for the last fifty years at least."

"You think maybe we'd better cut out the Turnover's Over Ball and the Three Quarters Party? I'll be hanged if I can stand a couple more flops. It's bad for general morale."

"You're taking this too seriously. Why not start working on the next shindig right now—you know —contests and such to have final playoffs at the party and such. Get them to start thinking about it. After all, you don't even know why there were so few . . . " The ping-ping-ping of a tiny bell indicated pilot-room intercom and Tim flipped a switch.

A plasticoid box on the wall spoke in Elbert Avery's dry tones. "Off duty now, Tim. You want to see me?"

Daneshaw spoke to the box on his desk, "Forsberg's here," he said. "You might come up and give us your opinion on the party. Were you there?"

"No, I was here. What happened, Arnie? The little ladies and gentlemen get rough over their grog?"

The recreation director twisted guiltily in his chair and muttered, "Wish they had!"

"No, El. Party seems to have been rather unpopular. You might canvass a bit on your way up and see if you can get a line on it. We'll have to cheer up Forsberg here if he's going to get back to keeping us gay."

The wall-box returned rather grumpily, "I trained for astrogator, not public relations. See you," and went dead.

ELBERT Avery cleared his communicator, glanced once more at the position-calc dials, rotated his chair and stood up. Slipping on his officer's braidjac, he nodded curtly to the Second Astrogator and went out into the corridor.

Twenty feet up the dark passage was the first of the eight rearward porthole stations. Avery slipped into the niche beside the observer's chair, and the watcher, sensing the astrogator's presence, shook his head vigorously against the hypnotic glitter of the stars and looked up. "How's it go?" from Avery.

"Go? Who's going anyplace? Stars sit still, we sit still just looking." Watcher Peters' voice was flat. "You sure anybody's going somewhere?"

Avery ignored the question. "Have a good time at the party last night?"

The watcher grunted, "Party, huh? All dressed up and no place to go. Same faces, same dining saloon, same games. I took a turn around the stations and went to bed. Party in this trap's just like looking out the hole. Nothing happens."

"Just don't like travel, eh?"

"Who said anything about travel? When you travel you move along all the time, and the trees and the mountains and towns rush past and you're going somewhere. I'll take travel any day—but this lost space hospital . . . "

Avery tried to be jovial. "Good thing we're old enough to be used to waiting. This would drive the young ones crazy."

"Driving me crazy too. Just waiting for the chance to be farmers and go on waiting for crops."

Avery edged out of the niche, although the watcher was obviously not done. "All settled down waiting to settle down. Coffee without sugar, night without end, months without news . . . " Avery was thirty feet down the corridor now. " . . . and no new audience to listen to all the swell gripes I sit here working out." His voice lost its flatness, became full and genial. "I'm the best damn griper in this damn outfit," he bragged, "I'm the . . . " (Noting Avery's absence) " . . . oh what the hell!" He brought his gaze back to the window to the stars.

Avery stopped at a door and rapped sharply. "Who is it?" "Elbert Avery." "Just a moment." He waited. "You can come in now." He turned the knob and opened the door. Angela Claflin half turned on the bench before her dressing table to face him. Her arms were raised and her hands were busy at the back of her head as she replaced the last of the bone pins in a great knot of hair black as a crow's wing. Tweezers, uncovered lipstick, rouge and powder boxes still lay on the table.

"Oh, Mustah Avery," in a voice a little high, a little twittery, "we missed you so at the pahty. We wuh so gay. Competition fo dancin' pahtnehs was jes furious and I was so hopin you'd come."

"I was on duty—couldn't make it."

"Oh I think that's jes cruel not to let jes everybody have some of the fun! You kin dance with me afteh suppah tomorr' night and we'll pretend the pahty's still on."

"I'll see." He stepped back toward the door.

"But Mistuh Avery, you didn' come hyar jes to listen to me chattuh. Is theh somethin you wanted?"

"Just dropped in to see if you enjoyed the party. Captain wanted to know."

"Well, bless his haht! You jes thank the cap'm fo me and tell him it's these yere social meetings that help us stay civilized an nice during this *long* trip." She giggled. "It makes a gihl downright unfemi-nine sometimes, studyin' manurin' problems and sheep-breedin."

"I'll tell him." He backed out and shut the door. "Downright unfemi-nine," he imitated softly, falsetto. "The old bat—dyed hair and all. No sense of the decorum of space—no sense, period." He walked on. "No loss, either."

HE hadn't intended to stop at Bart Westcott's room, but the door was open and he could hear voices. He pushed the door a little wider and went in.

Bart and Charlie Dean and Jeff Kuhnhardt in shirt-sleeves were sitting around a flat-top table covered with large papers in the middle of the room. Bart's left hand was swiping back his mop of reddish-grey hair, his right tapping excitedly with a sharp pencil at a far point on one of the papers. "We could put unit 84 over here in the middle of the back," he was saying emphatically, "which would leave more room for cupboards and the hatch to the storage attics."

Kuhnhardt was objecting less vigorously, "But that would cut out the center window and all the women say they want as many as possible. If you put 84 here," he pointed, "you'll have better passage of air from the conditioner through there." His pencil swept an arc across the paper.

Charlie Dean was the first to notice the newcomer. "Something we can do for you, Avery?" he asked briefly, setting down his pencil.

"Captain's compliments," he answered formally, "and he requests to know whether you enjoyed the Quarter-Way Party."

"Quarter-Way Party?" Charlie turned with a slightly puzzled look to his companions. "Oh, Quarter-Way Party . . . uh . . . return our compliments to the captain and tell him we loved it. Not that we were there, of course."

"A few more compliments and why not?"

"Too busy. These pre-fab housing units," he indicated the papers, "come in a couple thousand pieces like an unholy jig-saw puzzle. We've got to figure how to put them together and not have any left over to store and still not get the devil from the women who'll have to operate 'em."

"What's the rush? Still ten months to go."

"Well," Westcott looked a little sheepish, "it's got to be kind of fun. We've got to working out all the variations we can so each house will be some different from all the others. Then there are all the farm buildings and offices. We won't even have all the gimmicks worked out in ten months. Local Venus conditions, you know . . . "

"Sort of make work so the trip'll seem shorter?"

Kuhnhardt objected quickly, "As a matter of fact we could use another ten months. We never had time to complete our materials course on earth. We've got a lot of book work to do, too." He gestured toward Westcott's bunk, which was overflowing with manuals and thick volumes. "So parties are out, but we like them because we get fewer people in here looking for prospects for poker." He grinned at Avery.

There didn't seem to be any good comeback to this, so Avery just nodded and said, "Fine," and left. He took the elevator next to Wescott's room.

HE stopped the elevator halfway up to headquarters and got out. Better sample a few more responses to the party. No one answered his knock at the first two doors; the third was marked DARKROOM; but at the fourth he heard a sort of mumble and turned the knob.

Samuel Wyckoff was sitting on the edge of the bunk. Not a short man, but thin like all the healthy old ones: wispy white hair and faded blue eyes and a tremulous look about the mouth made him seem fragile. He was half-dressed; his thin long hands gripped the edge of the bunk; and he was staring at the floor a foot or two his side of the door.

"Going to bed early?" Elbert Avery was politely apologetic.

"No."

"Changing, then. It doesn't matter. Captain Daneshaw is having me ask around to find out how you people enjoyed the party last night. Did you have a good time?"

"A good time?" The man didn't seem to comprehend a simple question.

"That's it. Gayety, good time, fun, prizes and all, and sugar and cream in the coffee. Did you like it?"

"Didn't go." His gaze never left the floor, though it had moved to one side to avoid Avery's feet.

"Any particular reason? Program sound dull? Were you tired?"

"I guess so."

"You're probably working too hard. I just came from Westcott's room. He and a couple of other fellows are going it fast and furious on problems in architecture—as if they were trying to make their first billion the hard way. Relax, man. The United Assembly didn't mean us to work ourselves to death."

"What did they mean us to do?" Wyckoff asked with the first sign of interest.

Avery let loose one of his rare chuckles. "Who knows? They don't. Something impractical, you can be sure. But they didn't send us out to die. We cost 'em too much."

"More than we're worth." A statement.

"Of course. Billions, actually, and on some fool thing like this. You can't teach 'em. Government generations are too short. The only administration they care about is the last one and how to talk it down. It would take a major catastrophe to beat any sense into their heads."

"I suppose so." Wyckoff still stared at the floor.

"They didn't have any place for us in their set-up, and they aren't smart enough to figure out any. We know too much. The best they could come up with was this scheme to get us out of sight." Wyckoff was certainly a good listener. "They won't even know if we land safely for another two-three years when the ship does or doesn't come back for supplies. You'd think even the most moronic secretariat would know better than to send out a bunch of colonists that can't even multiply."

"But they sent us. They must have thought there was something we could do."

"We'll never know who sent us —or why. It's all mixed up with politics somewhere. Ours but to do as they say."

"Do or die."

"What? Oh . . . the quotation. Well, I stand corrected—don't know as it makes any great difference. We all will someday, in spite of the great Farrar and his coddling hospital."

Samuel looked even more fragile and a little wistful as he glanced up at Avery at last. "We thought this would be more interesting than the hospital, anyway."

"You don't like it?" El felt a sudden relief. Actually he didn't want to rob these people of any fun, he thought, and obviously most of them weren't having any anyway.

"It's just the same. Maybe we're too old to find it interesting. I dare say younger people . . . "

"Well, nobody can say it's our fault, anyhow. We didn't ask to get old any more than we asked to be born. I better go nose-side. Captain's waiting. Good night."

"Good night." Sam Wyckoff stood and followed Avery to the door. As it closed, he looked down at his unbuttoned shirt, his socks. "We didn't ask to get old," he whispered, and went back to the edge of his bunk.

AVERY hustled back to the elevator. He shouldn't have spent so much time talking. Wyckoff was a good fellow. Sometimes it seemed a darn shame that the government couldn't come up with something really good for old codgers like him. But what could you do with a superannuated book reviewer like Wyckoff? Old people ought to make good book reviewers and teachers. But naturally nobody'd listen to them. Those smart alecs in Washington wouldn't recognize a bear till it bit them. Only way to batter anything into their heads . . .

The elevator door opened and Avery swaggered truculently along the corridor to the headquarters anteroom, his fists clenched.

The captain and recreation director looked up at his entrance.

Captain Daneshaw greeted him. "Sorry to call you up here when you're off duty. This isn't really very serious." He smiled over at Forsberg.

"Well, I did what you wanted," Avery said, sitting down to face the recreation director at the large conference table. "I asked around to get the general reaction."

"And?" from Daneshaw.

"And . . . out of the six people I saw, only one woman—Miss Claflin, of course—just *luhved it,* had a *wondaful tahm.* The other five didn't go."

"Why?"

"One said it was monotonous. Said the whole trip was just like being in Block Nineteen only more so. Three fellows seemed to think it was too trivial to bother with. They've been making up better games with the housing blueprints, so they say. The last man said he was just tired." Avery leaned toward Forsberg. "Looks like you're going to have to make up a new game or think up some way to make 'em think they've never met each other and are just crazy to get acquainted." He snickered. "That's as I see it, of course. I'm no recreation director."

"Not bad!" Arnold Forsberg roared and slapped the table. "The man's a wizard, Captain!" He turned back to Avery. "You think I can't do it? The After Turnover Party theme is going to be New Personality. That's perfect! We'll announce it all over the ship the first thing tomorrow. Everybody's got eleven weeks to develop a new personality to wear on our new home, Venus. It's never too late to be somebody new. Be the man you've always wanted to be for the next hundred years. That's great!"

Avery tipped back in his chair during this blast. "It really sounds corny," he belittled. "We've had a century and a half to get like we are. Why change? I'm good enough for me."

"It's your idea," said the recreation director triumphantly, getting up, "and I like it. Sorry to have been a nuisance, Tim. I'll go straight to El Avery next time."

He buttoned his resplendent silver braidjac and came around the table, resting his hand fraternally on Avery's shoulder for a moment before he reached the door. "Good night. See you at the party." Then he was gone.

"NEED me for anything else tonight, Tim?" asked Avery.

"Thanks for doing the rounds, El," said Tim. "That's about all. By the way, who was the one you described as 'just tired'?"

"Oh, that was Wyckoff, Sam Wyckoff on the eighth floor."

"Any idea what tired him so much he didn't want to go to the party? I thought we were being pretty careful about fatigue. He's not one of the crew, is he?"

"No . . . kitchen helper maybe. He didn't say it was anything in particular. He did seem sort of shot, but he perked up and we had a good talk," added Avery.

"I see."

"Well, if that's all, I'll get along and eat and shoot a couple of games of slotto before I turn in. It's relaxing after sitting over a hot calculator all evening." At the door he turned. "Can't you join me this once?"

"Not tonight. Just a few more things to attend to, thanks."

After Avery left, Daneshaw straightened a few papers aimlessly on the dull green alloid table top. "Tired," he mused, "sort of shot. Might be a case for Doc Keighley. Better see to it. Of course, he might be homesick." He stood up and glanced around the piles of papers. Nothing that couldn't wait till tomorrow.

In three minutes, he was knocking briskly on Wyckoff's door.

There was no answer. Surely the man hadn't gotten to sleep in the twenty minutes since Avery talked to him. He knocked again. Some sort of mumble came from inside. Tim turned the knob and walked in.

The light in the cabin was off, but in the dim reflection from the corridor walls, Tim could see Wyckoff was lying in the bunk, which faced the door, on his back with the covers pulled up under his chin. "Asleep so soon, Sam?" asked Tim in a low voice.

"Not quite. What is it?"

"El Avery was just up. Said you looked exhausted and naturally I was a little worried. Had a check-up with the doctor recently?"

"No . . . no . . . don't worry about me," faintly.

"That's part of my job. We want everybody to get to Venus ready for a hard pull. Have you been studying too hard on the trip?"

"No. My job's not very important. Please don't worry about me."

"Mind if I turn on the light and have a little talk?" Tim reached for the switch of the reading lamp at the head of the bunk on his right.

"If you want to," reluctantly.

Tim clicked the switch and sat down on the foot of the bunk. "Finding the trip comfortable?" he smiled.

"I . . . I suppose."

"Miss the pretty nurses back at the hospital?"

"Oh no."

Tim looked down at the edge of the bunk thoughtfully. "Been eating regularly? Sleeping . . . say, did you spill something on the blanket?" he asked suddenly and reached forward to touch the small dark stain just above the edge of the bunk. The stain was wet.

TIM grabbed the blanket and stripped it back. Wyckoff was still wearing his undershirt and slacks and the red stain was bright on the white sheets above and below his left wrist.

Tim jumped up and pulled open the top drawer of the built-in wall-chest, ripped out a handkerchief and hair brush and had a tourniquet on Wyckoff's upper arm before the man in the bunk could make a movement.

Holding the hair brush tight in his right hand, Tim reached across the bunk and lifted Wyckoff's other hand. There was no blood there. He sat back on the edge of the bunk.

"You meant to do this, Sam?" Daneshaw's voice was reproachful.

"I guess so . . . I don't know."

"I don't think you do know. Because you're not a coward, Sam. You're not really afraid to do your share for the rest of us on this trip. We need all of us."

"Oh, I'm not very important."

"We can't spare you," Tim replied positively. "But we can talk about that in a few minutes. Can I trust you to hang on to this brush?"

"I guess so."

Tim released his grip when he felt Wyckoff's firm hold on the handle. He darted into the tiny laboratory and opened the medicine cabinet. The bulb in the interior glowed softly through the few plastic articles on the shelves. Tim rummaged among the soapaks and found a small glass bottle of aspirillin tablets. Grasping it by the neck, he struck it smartly against the monel basin, shattering it into the basin and onto the floor. He dropped the neck among the tablets in the basin and went back to the top drawer of the chest where he found another handkerchief. Back at the bunkside, he sopped up as much blood as he could with the cloth, then took it back to the lavatory and wrung out a little on the floor, wadded the handkerchief and tossed it into the basin.

Approaching Wyckoff, who had sat up in the bunk, he pushed him down again gently. "You push your button for the steward and get the doctor right away. Tell him you dropped the aspirillin bottle and got cut by a piece of flying glass. "I'm going to wait in the darkroom next door and come back for a long talk after the doc is done. Hear me?"

"Yes."

"Because if the doctor doesn't come in five minutes, I'm going for him and the psychiatrist, too. But I think you'd rather not have this get out any more than I would."

"No."

"All right, then. Push the button."

Daneshaw waited while Wyckoff pushed the button in the wall above his right elbow. Then he hurried out of the cabin and into the next door, the darkroom where the biological photographer would do his work after the landing on Venus until the building was completed. He left the door open a crack and waited for the approach of the steward and doctor.

He leaned noiselessly, suddenly weary, against the wall of the darkroom. Here was the problem of the hospital all over again. Was it his fault somehow? The trip had been a great victory, seemingly, over the sagging spirits of his friends, his "army." (He heard the steward go in and come out.) His head seemed full of whirring thoughts without meaning. What fear, what despair had got into the man? What was it . . . how did the words go?

. . . pluckt from us all hope of due reliefe,
That earst us held in love of lingering life;
Then hopelesse hartlesse, gan the cunning thiefe
Perswade us die, to stint all further strifes
To me he lent this rope, to him a rustie knife.

How could Wyckoff have felt that life was too much to bear? The thought was so simple once it seemed right . . .

What if some little paine the passage have,
That makes fraile flesh to feare the bitter wave?
Is not short paine well borne, that brings long ease . . .

(The door to Sam's cabin opened and closed again.) He would have to talk like an angel or a devil to stop Sam from another try. But Sam was one of his people and he'd got them all into this. *His* responsibility . . . his.

TIM had a sudden guilty feeling he had dozed off when he heard the door open and close for the third time. The doctor must have gone. He came out of the darkroom and re-entered Wyckoff's.

Sam was sitting on the edge of the bunk regarding his bandaged wrist wryly.

"All fixed up?"

"I expect so."

"Was it bad?"

"No. He didn't even have to take stitches—just little tape strips." The wry look became a grimace. "Said I was lucky it didn't get the artery. I can't even cut my wrist the right way."

Tim grinned. If Sam's sense of humor was returning, it might not be such a hard job. "Aren't you supposed to be lying down?"

"I don't think so."

"Well, you lie down anyhow and let's talk about things." Sam lowered himself obediently and Daneshaw went on. "First I want to know if you're in any trouble? Had a row with anybody? Think you've done something you wish you hadn't?"

"Well . . . no."

"Good. Now what's your job on board and what do you do after we land?"

"Just a kitchen helper here. When we get there, I'll run the control panels for some remotracs—planting and harvesting, you know."

"Not a very exciting set of jobs. How's the kitchen."

The slender man bristled, looked less frail. "They don't like the way I peel wathros. Mrs. Kaplan says I peel all the vitamins off. She says you can't trust a man with a peeler anyhow," he added fiercely. "And I hate wathros no matter how you peel them!"

Tim sighed.

"You're in a rut, Sam. You've worn out that job. And you and Mrs. Kaplan are evidently wearing out each other. Do you want to change jobs?"

"Oh, I don't know. I don't mean anything against Mrs. Kaplan. She does a good piece of work."

"So should you, and wathro peeling's not necessarily it." Tim mused for a moment. "Are you sure the doc didn't say anything about your staying in bed?"

"No. I'm sure he didn't even mention it."

"It probably never occurred to him you'd do anything else. Anyhow I think this would be a good time for a little excursion. Have you been all over the ship?"

"Not since the big tour before blast-off."

"Get your shirt and shoes on. We'll go the rounds and you can have your pick of the jobs. You look them all over tonight and make up your mind tomorrow which one you would like."

Wyckoff sat up and Tim slung him the shirt from the back of the chair. He had to help him with the snaps on the shirt and the shoes, but in a few moments they were out in the corridor.

"You shouldn't spend all this time on me, Mr. Daneshaw. You just pick out a job and I'll take it."

"Spending time *is* my job and you need a job you'll like. You know, Sam, emotional conflicts can wear a man to a frazzle twenty times faster than hard labor. And don't call me Mister. I'm Tim to everybody unless they want to bawl me out for something, and Captain only when they want me to bawl somebody else out."

"All right, Tim. Let's go."

Tim grasped Sam's arm and hit his long stride. He'd get more from him on the way. Emotional responses sure could knock hell out of a man.

HELL or something seemed knocked out with the insistent "Ting, ting-ting" of the rising chime in the captain's cabin at seven the next morning.

First waking. Waking itself seemed a great exertion this time. Then the long, long pause of gentle thought, of mustering of energies before opening his eyes and making a physical move to rise. Tim Daneshaw's first thought was of sinking to sleep again, of overwhelming fatigue. The bunk was firmer than usual—seemed to thrust up against his body, and to thrust up again, wearyingly, like a wave. The association brought words . . .

. . . *Is there any peace*

In ever climbing up the climbing
wave?
All things have rest, and ripen
toward the grave
In silence; ripen, fall and ceases
Give us long rest or death, dark
death, or dreamful ease.

Full consciousness came like a blow. Death, dark death meant Wyckoff, of course; and Wyckoff would be coming this morning, or, if he didn't, he, Tim Daneshaw must go in search . . . must fight . . . poor Sam Wyckoff deserved work . . . Tim felt his thought grow dizzy and the lift and lift under him gave way to a fall and fall. He opened his eyes.

The room was steady. Only the feeling of falling a little, then stopping, then falling a little continued. Tim brought his eyes down to the desk top again and again, each time to see the glowing desk lamp, pencils, papers, opened book lie quiet, steady, without tremor. The motion must be in his dizzying head. The cabin beyond the desk was in shadow, but the shadow retreated and advanced in rhythm with the falling.

By a tremendous effort, Tim raised his hand to the wall button and pushed. The hand fell back limp on the covers.

Why are we weighed upon with heaviness?

His mind revolved dully, waiting for an answer, waiting for the steward, waiting and turning and almost dozing.

To answer the gentle knock on the door was too hard. He could turn his head a little. After a sharper knock, the door opened and Steward Loomis looked in. "Everything all right, Captain?" No answer.

Loomis came over to the bunk quickly. "Tim, what's the matter?"

"Hello, Loo. Weak, I guess." Words came easier now. "Better get Doc Keighley."

"You bet I will," and the steward was already hurrying out the door. "You stay right there," he added firmly and unnecessarily.

Tim stayed right there. The bed stopped falling, but he didn't move. He knew how to relax from years of practice in the hospital and years of habit before that.

Keighley walked in, bag in hand, without knocking and came and sat on the edge of the bunk. "Tim?"

"Hello, Doc. I feel done in. Air supply all right?"

"Air's OK," Doc's hand felt Tim's forehead, reached for his wrist, his eye recording the sweep of the second hand on the desk chrono. A few moments later his stethoscope pressed against Tim's chest.

IN answer to Keighley's probing questions, Tim described his symptoms. The doctor rummaged in his bag for a hypo-pak and ampulle. After the shot, he took out a bottle of capsules, closed his bag and drew up the chair from the desk.

"You know, Tim," he began softly, "we're both *old* men. We can keep going indefinitely as long as the rate is slow and steady. Acceleration is mighty dangerous. Now you're going to rest."

" . . . could stand a few days of taking it easy . . ."

"Not a few days—months. Flat in bed."

"But the ship . . . the people . . . " The vision of Samuel Wyckoff rose again.

"The crew and the Lord can take care of the ship; we people will have to take care of ourselves. We'll need you more the last few months of flight and after we land. If you've got to see anybody, I'll get them right now before that sedative takes effect."

Tim's hand rose and fell. "All right, Doc," the thin, exhausted voice fell too, "Even Moses didn't make the Promised Land."

"You'll make it, you fuddleheaded old Moses, if you obey Doc Keighley's commandments. Even Moses had more sense than to try to be captain and master of ceremonies and life of the party and general trouble shooter all at once."

Daneshaw smiled wanly. "I'll be good. Better have El Avery come up before I go to sleep. He'll have to take on some of my duties or figure out somebody else. He knows as much about the ship as anybody. Don't worry him, though, Frank. He's a nervous old dog . . . By the way, can I read?"

"You can't even hold a book for a couple of weeks at least. If you want to hear something, I'll send you a reader or you can have a player and a bunch of wires if we carry anything but treatises on farming. I wouldn't be surprised if Avery'd make a good top man—more autocratic, less tolerant than you, but there are more ways of killing a cat . . . and I'll assign you nurses in six hour shifts. It'll keep some of the girls out of mischief."

"Frank . . . have a heart!"

"You have one—and hang onto it." Doc Keighley gathered up his bag and left the cabin.

Outside the door he almost bumped into Jack White, Second Astrogator, and Steward Loomis. "Loo, get El Avery up here right away before the hypo hits him. Jack, you go in and sit with him till Avery gets here. He's all right, boys. Just worn out. Let everybody know he'll be back on deck after turnover—*if* you all stay out of his way till then. Don't let anybody but Avery or the nurse in, Jack," and the little doctor bustled off and out of sight around the curve of the corridor.

TO Jack White, entering the tiny cabin lit only by the desk lamp, Tim Daneshaw looked near gone.

He went over and sat silent on the chair the doctor had turned to the bunk. Tim's eyes were shut, but he spoke weakly.

"El? El Avery?"

"No Captain, it's Jack White. Avery will be here as soon as he can."

A long silence.

Daneshaw spoke again. "Got to shift command, Jack."

"Yes, sir."

"What about Avery, Jack. Can he do it?"

"I think so. You remember how he handled that gyroscope record the first two weeks out."

"How was that, Jack?"

White was startled, but gave no sign. If Tim Daneshaw's memory was slipping, he really was in bad shape. "You remember, Captain. We were only a few thousand miles out when the gyro appeared to be recording a constant correction, and how Mister Avery," (a term of deference would show Tim how respected Avery was) "was so thorough and kept the crew so busy they didn't have time to worry about the real danger of being off course. He got the engineers doing radionic soundings of the walls of the big tube in action and some of the crew went practically into the dead tubes looking for flare action. He had everybody else who knew about it testing all over the inner skin for an air leak that might be producing a tiny jet. It was wonderful the way he got the passengers thinking it was a routine check for the early stages of any space trip. And he never let down—sat at the calculators eighteen hours a day until he found out that the recording pen on the gyro must have got bent in blast-off. We were proud of him, Captain."

"I recall it now. You think he'll make a good executive?" Tim seemed pitifully eager for assurance.

"Make an executive, Captain? He is an executive. He's the Old Fox of Avery, Inc. again, since those two weeks. He's taken to coming into the pilot room when he's off duty —just coming in and standing and watching as if he wanted to keep an eye on everything and everybody. And nobody seems to resent it. And he never needles the rest of us button-pushers when he finds an error in calculations. We all make them, El too, but we've quit deviling each other about them since then. He's your man."

"Thanks, Jack. I . . . hoped . . . you'd . . . feel . . . " Tim's voice trailed off. "Tired . . . get Avery . . . tell him Sam Wyckoff . . . "

Another silence.

"Captain Daneshaw?"

No answer.

"Tim!" White was more insistent.

A gentle rap on the door.

"Tim, are you awake?"

After a moment of silence, Jack White got to his feet and tiptoed out.

Avery was on the other side of the door.

"He's asleep, El," White informed him. "Very sick—heart. Doc Keighley was here and says he'll be in bed at least till turnover. He told me that you were to take command—Tim Daneshaw, that is."

The two men moved away from the closed door. Elbert Avery turned to face White. "What's that about command?" he asked sharply.

"He wants you to take over. Thinks you're the best man for it. Likes the way you handled the passengers and crew over the gyro business."

"Fine job I'd make of awarding bridge prizes and settling arguments between second and third cooks on how much salt in the buns." Avery sounded gruff but pleased.

"Orders are orders," Jack White forced a smile.

"Then I guess I'll have to order you back to my turn of duty in the pilot room while I get my bearings."

"El?" Jack was struck with a memory. "The captain said something about Sam Wyckoff, too. He went to sleep before he finished. You better ask him about it next time you see him."

"Here he comes now." The frail figure came slowly, deliberately around the curve of the corridor. "Tim probably wanted him to help me out. I hear he took him around the ship for some reason last night."

SAMUEL Wyckoff's eyes regarded the floor of the corridor as he approached. If the other men had not moved out of his way and spoken, he would probably have continued his progress to the captain's door without noticing them.

"Sam . . . Sam Wyckoff. It's not that bad. Doc says he'll be up and around after turnover." Jack White's voice was full of concern.

Wyckoff looked up. "What?" he asked dully.

Avery repeated, "It's not too bad. Doctor Keighley says he has to rest but he'll be back on his feet in less than three months if we don't get him worried or tired again. That right, Mr. White?"

"That's it. And the captain said something about you just as he was dozing off. Mr. Avery here says he thinks he meant for you to help out in the emergency."

"He took you all over the ship last night, didn't he?" added Avery.

"Well, yes . . . but . . . "

"He must have had some idea of what was coming. I've never been in half the labs or the kitchen and Ole Sorensen wouldn't let me nearer to his prize cows than the door of the stable. Not that I'm fond of cows, anyway. So if I've got to take over command for a while, looks as if you're the choice of the boss for liason man. C'mon along up to the confab room and we'll pow-wow."

"But . . . I . . . , that is . . . can't I see the captain? He said . . . I mean I need to see him. He told me to come this morning." Wyckoff looked from one to the other.

White was definite. "Not today, maybe not this week. Doctor's orders. You better get along with Mr. Avery. You know the ship. The captain would want you to keep things running smoothly without a break."

"Well, all right, I'll come." Wyckoff sounded doubtful still, but he allowed the others to lead him toward the elevator which would take them up to headquarters.

Just at the elevator door they were met by the floor steward, Loomis.

"Mr. Avery?"

"Yes."

"Who's to be in command, sir?"

"I am."

"Well, Mrs. Jeffries of the laundry just phoned and said when she got down to the laundry a few minutes ago the place was flooded with water. One of the taps sprung or something, and she called damage control and they told her to call water reclamation and I guess the water-rec squad was all over at hydroponics trying to figure out why the increase in humidity—anyhow, Mrs. Jeffries is upset because she can't get the captain and will you go down and smooth her out?" Loomis recited rapidly.

Avery turned to Samuel Wyckoff. "Guess you get right into harness. This is for you." Then to Loomis, "Sam's my righthand man for just this sort of thing. Give him all the help you can," and back to Wyckoff: "We'll see you up nose-side as soon as you're through. We've got to plan fast so's not to upset the whole crowd. You take the elevator down; we'll walk up. We're in no hurry."

As the elevator glided down out of sight past the transplast door, and Loomis returned along the corridor, Avery and White turned into the narrow winding stair to climb slowly to the fourth floor above. White looked up at Avery's back and asked, puzzled, "Do you think this came on suddenly? And why? I didn't see him too often, but he always seemed so tough, so . . . well . . . resilient, if you know what I mean. But he must have known it was coming if he took Wyckoff around last night. What do you think happened to him?"

The man ahead shrugged his shoulders and they climbed on and up.

THE "New-Side Out Ball and Social Assembly" was in full swing the night after Turnover, when Jack White edged quickly through the door into the circular Great Salon just in time to avoid collision with a fantastically costumed guest carrying a tray half full of tiny crystal coffee-glasses, and stood peering through the half-dark of lowered lights at the little clusters of people in easy chairs and loungettes which ringed the room and filled it with a confusion of talk and laughter. He moved a step or two away from the wall, his eyes seeking more intently through the small throng near the center of the room on his right where Captain Daneshaw, guarded by a solicitous Sam Wyckoff, sat in a great raised chair receiving congratulations on his recovery. Elbert Avery was not in that bunch. Mr. White picked his way to the left where a few couples were dancing to the slow strains of the xerxia being played by a small orchestra on a bit of a curtailed stage. So intent was his search, that he ran into the arm of a chair and almost fell into the midst of the gay little groups.

Helen Platt's voice was sweet, chiding, "You're quite out of character, Mister White. You have to give up the absent-minded math professor this evenin. We're all somebody new tonight, you know.

Scattered laughter.

White looked down. The ex-Latin teacher, heavily made up, had hidden her thinning grey hair under a towering bejewelled turban. "I'm a movie actress and Phil here is a big game hunter," she added, swinging a ruby-shod toe toward a lamp-bronzed man wearing a chalk-white nilene tropojak and encircling crimson commerbund. "Tell us something about yourself and let us guess what kind of secret you've been hiding the last century."

White forced a smile. "Not yet," he apologized. "Got to find Elbert Avery first. Quite urgent. Is he around here?"

Nobody had seen him, and Jack White, promising abstractedly to come back later and let them "guess him" went on down the room, cautiously avoiding another accident.

From circle to cluster he repeated his question with no better success. Several times he was asked why he wanted Avery and twice men of the group offered to help him hunt. To each question, he mumbled something about its not being important —he just wanted to find El Avery for a minute, thanks, and went on toward the orchestra on its stage. As he made his way carefully around the room, peering at dancers, at circles on the other side of the party dusk, he failed to notice the silence behind him. The worried glances which followed him, the half sentences, "Avery this time?" "Overwork . . . " "Too much for one man . . . " " . . . collapsed somewhere?'" " . . . do you suppose?" " . . . something wrong, definitely . . . " "Did you see how pale Jack was?" failed to reach him; but more than a quadrant of the hall was aware of his quickened pace when he caught sight of the wiry little man standing against the wall half hidden by the outer edge of one curtain of the stage.

ELBERT Avery was regarding the dancers morosely, his full-dress uniform indicating that he, at least, was sticking to his character as chief astrogator in preference to some more exotic role. As he had expressed it to Samuel Wyckoff when both men went to escort Tim Daneshaw triumphantly to the assembly, "I'm too old to change again. I'm an astrogator now and a 'gator I'll be to the bitter end."

Jack White reached him now, spoke in low tones; and both men hurried out a small door at the side of the hall. A sigh seemed to go over the room and conversation rose to a new pitch of animation in a dozen places when it was obvious that Avery was in full control of his wind and limbs.

Out in the curving corridor, White took Avery's arm and fairly swept him back to the left, to the elevator. He could hardly speak. "Gyroscope bearings worn on one side . . . Powell and North rechecking porthole readings after turnover . . . degrees out of course . . . miss Venus completely as we're headed . . . " he almost babbled.

Avery pulled back abruptly against White's arm and stopped dead. "Get your breath, man," he snapped, "and tell me clearly what's wrong. Something about the course?"

A paper-tophatted guest with a tray of filled glasses of ebony coffee, unable to pass them as they stood in the middle of the corridor, waited behind for them to move on before he could reach the door to the Saloon twenty feet farther on . . . waited listening.

"Preposterous!" shouted Avery, "we've had watchers with accurate charts peeling their eyes at the sky every foot of the way till now."

"We're going to miss, I tell you," White responded desperately. He began to tremble as the delayed effects of shock started to tell, and grabbed Avery's arm to steady himself, then pulled Avery toward the shaft and into the car. "Come down and see for yourself. We're lost! Lost!"

The tophatted tray carrier continued to the door of the Saloon. Setting his tray on the floor just inside, he circled the room, pausing at each cozy gathering to recount White's frantic statements and passing on to the next like a man in a dream.

"NONSENSE, nonsense," Avery was gently shaking the already trembling man in the elevator. "Nobody's lost among the inner planets. I'll come down with you. You'll see . . . a little button pushing . . . " As if to illustrate, he pushed the button and the car began to descend.

The top-hatted figure didn't come to the group containing Dr. Marquith, the psychiatrist, until it had covered two-thirds of the room. The doctor questioned him carefully—this could be another breakdown like several which had occurred early in the trip when port-watchers, eyes fatigued and brain a-dazzle from watching the heavens, had declared positively that the ship had left the solar system altogether and had required days of treatment to convince them that their fears or concealed desires were of the shadowy substance of dreams. But the waiter showed none of the symptoms of such a breakdown.

"I think we'd better tell your story to the captain, son," the doctor suggested quietly to the now haggard looking older man. "There is certainly nothing you or I can do to help matters and there is no need to alarm the rest of the passengers now." He led the unprotesting man toward Daneshaw on his dais.

They watched the group around the captain disperse at some word from the doctor; their tension mounted as the psychiatrist talked to Daneshaw and Wyckoff; and the hatted man gestured toward the door through which he had entered the room.

When Samuel Wyckoff straightened up from leaning over Captain Daneshaw, absolute quiet preceded the first of his clear confident tones.

"Matt Carey, here, wants me to tell you that he's awfully sorry he alarmed you. He did overhear Mr. White tell Mr. Avery something which sounded . . . well . . . disturbing. But we must all realize that many a slight accident has seemed disastrous at its first reporting. And we haven't even had an official report of any kind."

A woman somewhere began to sob.

"Come now," Wyckoff said reproachfully, "we are not children!"

A nervous giggle sounded from another quarter.

Wyckoff continued more forcefully. "Dr. Marquith, Carey and I are going down to the pilot room to find out what we can for you, so keep your shirts (I mean costumes) on, and don't forget to make Captain Daneshaw's recovery celebration a gay as well as a memorable one." He patted Tim's shoulder familiarly, beckoned to the two others to precede him across the floor.

At the door, he saw the tray of glasses and turned. "You fellows better bring another round of drinks. I could stand one myself." He stooped, lifted a glass, drank, and followed the others out.

Men rose automatically from the groups, collecting empty and half-ful glasses alike, and headed in a mass for the door; but the first few attempts to revive conversation sounded so loud that when the room finally filled with sound, it was the rustle and sibilance of whispering.

THE self-appointed investigating committee of three stood in the pilot-room door.

El Avery's crisp voice was snapping at White the new equation to be set into the B calculator, rattling out the key for the data Powell handed him to be fed to C by North in the intervals of rest while A calculator assimilated and digested. The floor of the computation area was littered with the yards of coils of paper ribbon Avery had ripped from the roll of gyro record to find the original deviation (minus the bits which Carruthers, Fifth Astrogator, had taken to the enlargement room for micro-measurements). At the accepted break for complete clearing of the A calculator banks, Avery's precision broke to a growl.

"Damned earthbound whelps!" he muttered. "Don't even bother to discover major factors like light pressure in their measly little tubs!" He jerked to a stand, stripped off his braidjak and flung it into the midst of the insubstantial paper snake. He sat down with a thump and bent back over the calculator keyboard. "Those babies don't care what they lose or how!"

He set to work again with White's eighth set of solutions forming them into factors of equations of his own. Powell, passing around the welter of paper, was the first to notice the observers and yelled at them "You boys round up the engine room crew, quick. Get them into the boom room and tell 'em to stand by for intermittent rocket and main tube fire! Beat it!"

Jack White looked up from his keyboard, "And get the passengers into bed for turnover, too!'"

"You take Matt, Doc," said Wyckoff, authoritatively. "Don't make an announcement, just go the rounds and call out engine crew as if it were a piece of routine. Matt, you stand out in the hall and tell them there to report to the boom room presto. When you get 'em all out, Doc, go and tell Tim Daneshaw I'll be down to report in a minute. Jolly 'em up a bit if you can."

Wyckoff himself advanced a couple of steps into the pilot room. Powell passed him again on his way back to the massive data spitter and said, "Thought we asked you to clear out."

His rudeness seemed not to affect the easy poise of the slim old man. Wyckoff's voice was conciliatory, "I've got to make some sort of report on this beehive to the captain. It's the general impression that we're in the middle of disaster."

Powell roared, "Avery! Who let this out? The passengers are rioting!"

"Not rioting—praying more likely," corrected the man at the door.

"That'll keep 'em out of trouble," Avery flipped back, his pencil moving feverishly across a scratch pad.

Wyckoff called across the clatter of the spitter, now operating with a ferocious din, "What'll we tell 'em, Avery? They've got to know something or there will be a riot or worse. Is there really any danger?"

"There's always danger," Avery was growling again, "when some unmitigated unweaned engineers on an unmentionable planet cook up a foolproof system of astrogation."

He handed the scratch pad to Jack White and waved a hand at A calculator. "Take off these and add them into the firing times. I'll send Wilman and Adams up and put them on the intercom for porthole reports during firing. I'm going with Sam and stop the rush for the life-boats we don't have."

Donning his jak, he arose and kicked his way defiantly through the welter of paper and stamped free of it as he reached the door. He hurried up the corridor to the elevator, eight or ten paces in advance of Wyckoff, and jabbed the button. "Sam my boy," he barked impatiently, waiting for the car, "the worst cause of panic is panic. I've been on the market and I know!"

THE elevator door slid shut and Wyckoff repeated his earlier question, "Is it really bad, El?"

"Probably nothing a little prompt action can't fix," Avery replied. "It's going to take two more turnovers, though. You know we haven't any jets in the nose to amount to anything, and we'll have to tack back across our charted course like bats out of you know where. Carruthers will have to whip up a new batch of charts for the sky-watchers, too, but we can still outsmart those idiots on earth and land on Venus *if* we want to."

"If we *want* to?" The car stopped and the two got out.

"I said if we want to, and that's what I meant," Avery replied tartly, heading up the Saloon floor corridor. "I'll bet most of us didn't want or expect much more than to cut loose from our old lives and problems; and that's completely accomplished. Most of us just wanted to crawl away and die with some decent measure of privacy. We can do that, too, if we want to."

Through the thin panel of the saloon door the music came, singing weakly at first, then growing, tremulously . . .

Eternal Father, God of Grace,
Whose hand hath set the stars in place,

"We've changed our minds, Elbert," said Samuel Wyckoff.

Who biddst the planets turn and sweep
To Thine appointed orbits keep,
Oh hear us when to Thee we cry
For those in peril in the sky!

A moment's silence through the door. Wyckoff pushed it open for Avery and followed him into the room.

The hundreds of people standing in the room, looking at Captain Daneshaw in the center, did not notice the two until they had almost reached him. Hundreds of breaths, thousands of muscles clenched, they awaited the word. Avery gave one furtive, almost guilty look around at the staring faces; then, his jauntiness returning, he took the last few steps to the captain's side. Tim Daneshaw raised his hand, unnecessarily, for silence. Avery spoke.

"With your assistance, we shall land on Venus on schedule."

A great sigh from hundreds of lips.

Avery continued, "We are off course because of a factor that was overlooked in building the *Colonia*. But there is no reason why we can't meet our new home when she gets there. There is no reason why we can't do a better job than the engineers and Space Commission expected of us." *No* reason. There were more ways of outsmarting young fools than tying their feet with high tension wire. He gestured at Sam Wyckoff. "Tell 'em what to do next, trouble shooter."

Wyckoff took up, "There will be two more turnovers, the first within a couple of hours, I expect. You've just been through one and know what to do as far as remaining in your cabins with a good supply of solid food in your kits and plenty of packaged water. As Mr. Avery expresses it, we shall have to run to catch up with our course, so there will be acceleration, too. The gravitators will be switched on again immediately after turnover, but, since acceleration may be intermittent the ship may seem bumpy until a constant acceleration has been reached. All of you who are not essential crew or involved with food service or care of animals had better go for rations at once and then strap into your bunks with a sedative and maybe a good book. Food services go hand out ration packs and report back here. Crew members still in the hall meet with Mr. Avery by the stage." He paused for breath. "And before you walk not run to the nearest food hatch," (tension in the Great Saloon was a new thing, alert, responsive), "let's have three rousing cheers for a better man with a calculator than any on earth! Hip! Hip! . . . "

"Hoo-ray!" Deafening.

"Hip! . . . Hip! . . ."

"Hoo-ray!"

The third cheer was a wave of noise that had no beginning but dimmed suddenly when a woman near the captain folded her hands and bowed her head. The crowd followed the example like one being.

Avery, too, bowed his head for

a moment, fierce triumph fading from his face; then he strode down the floor to the stage as the throng moved in orderly departure to the doors around the room, a man here and there following him.

Tim Daneshaw grasped Sam Wyckoff's hand with a quick, friendly shake. *"Grow old along with me, The best is yet to be,"* he quoted musingly; and both men followed the little line leading the way to Avery and action.

THE END

THE HYDRAULIC ACCUMULATOR

SOME years ago we took recognition of a little gadget which was making its awareness known to industry—the hydraulic accumulator. It is one of those simple inventions—apparently—which has a profound effect on mechanical devices generally. It's about time we took another look at it—not only with regard to what it is doing or will be doing shortly—but what its uses will be thirty years from now.

The hydraulic accumulator is nothing more or less than a rubber bag full of compressed gas! It is a convenient device for storing large amounts of energy slowly and releasing it rapidly.

It consists of a metal cylinder—very strong—within which is a rubber or synthetic rubber bag, filled with an inert gas like nitrogen. A metal tube leads to one end of the cylinder. When oil is pumped through the tube into the cylinder it compresses the gas in the bag. A small pump can do the job slowly, each stroke compressing the gas further. When the desired pressure is attained the pump is shut off and a valve closed. Stored within the steel cylinder in the form of the potential energy of compressed gas, is a tremendous amount of energy which can be released slowly or rapidly. This energy can be transmitted through a piston and levers, to do practically anything from lowering the landing gear of planes to lowering the windows of cars, opening the trunk, the hood, or what have you. Just name the job; the hydraulic accumulator can do it.

It's best known among machine tool builders and aircraft designers. But it's making its way into every field. You might summarize its general effect by saying that it's a gadget which operates on the principle that a little work done for a long time equals a lot of work done for a short time.

Spaceships—well, come closer to our own time—jet and rocket planes—require large amounts of power for operating such things as doors, airlocks, motor mechanisms, guns, and many other things. They can't carry big motors and generators to do everything. But they can carry a small motor and pump—plus an hydraulic accumulator.

And so it clearly shows that the most prosaic devices have an important role in the field which is coming—rocketry and space flight. We're laying the foundation for these advances with crude bricks, but it won't be long before the superstructure is added.

BOTTLE PILOTS

You're at seventy thousand feet. You glance at the instrument panel and you see the needle on six hundred—six hundred per hour! In your sleek pressurized canopied cockpit you don't even sense the terrific knife-edged wind that would peel the paint from your wings—if they were painted.

The mighty roar of the jets sounds to your ears like the faintest whisper and only a slight trembling of the plane betrays the fact that the motors are running.

Suddenly your eye is caught by the brief flare of red before your eyes and the acrid odor of hot oil hits your nose. You know something's wrong. For a short moment you're panic stricken. Then reason takes over. You watch the panel. The bolometers show rising temperatures. You know you're on fire!

Hastily you make your decision. You've got to go out into the racing hell of bitter-thin air outside. You shove the nose down in a steep dive to lose altitude as fast as possible.

You press the transmitter stud. "I'm jettisoning — 4QX—all out!" You don't wait for the reply. Your finger seeks the firing stud. You brace yourself against the shock. You touch the stud. There's a sharp crack as the binding rivets explode —and cleanly you and your surrounding shell are thrown far from the burning jet. And seated comfortably in the housing of metal and plastic which surrounds you, supplied with oxygen from the bottles, you fall free until the barometric trippers trigger off the parachute at the right altitude. You've abandoned ship. . . .

The preceding isn't an exaggeration. In today's superspeed rockets and jets, abandoning them is as dangerous as riding them down. The U.S. services, improving on the cartridge-ejected cockpit have gone even farther. No man can live very long at high altitudes, terrific wind speeds, low pressures and without oxygen. He must be bottled in a cocoon. And so when the time to abandon a jet plane comes, the entire pilot housing, a self-sufficient world for a few minutes, is ejected by explosive bullets which throw it clear of the descending ship.

For minutes the pilot-carrying cocoon falls free until the air becomes thick enough for a parachute to take hold. The bitter cold of the upper atmosphere is left, the shattering low pressures no longer exist. A man can now live. The parachute flips out, and like a baby dangling in a harness the pilot of the plane floats to Earth.

No man could possibly withstand the terrific wind pressures which would literally rip the flesh and skin from his body if he dared to fall free from a six hundred mile an hour jet. He's got to be protected. And when the age of rocket flight becomes common, the problem will be that much more intensified. Well, the solution has been found. Bottle up a man and he can resist anything.

THE BRAVE WALK ALONE

By John McGreevey

DIRK Jemson pressed his forehead against the cool metal of the astro-chart and hoped that he was not going to be sick. At any moment, the space cruiser would be entering the gravity field of Caliban, and if he were ordered to assume control . . . he shuddered at the prospect.

Around him in the cabin, the other members of the crew went quietly about their duties. Allen, the astrogator worked over his charts and calculations; Kennedy, the atochanic squinted worriedly at the readings on his gauges; Tabor, the biophysicist was engrossed in a book.

They were men handling routine assignments automatically. If they felt any of the fear, the impending nausea which constricted Dirk's stomach, they gave no outward indication of it.

He straightened himself and closed his eyes. These others were at home out in space, unperturbed by the thought that they were rushing now at the speed of light toward an unknown world, the dark

Illustrated by Bill Terry

He was a coward not only in the eyes of his men but his father as well. Yet sometimes fear can be mistaken for the honor badge of great courage. . . .

satellite of Caliban. They could not understand this space sickness which held him in a vise. They were like his father.

Dirk looked apprehensively toward the audio-visor above Allen's head. Momentarily, his father's face would blur into that screen; his father's voice would saw into the quiet of the cabin with a command. And all of these men would come to attention and listen, for this would be the face and voice of Commandant Jemson—Terra's most renowned and daring space explorer.

Dirk's gaze roamed the cabin. These others — Allen, Kennedy — even Tabor who was only an observer—would listen to the words of the Commandant; but they would know that his message was meant only for Dirk. Dirk Jemson—the Commandant's son.

Wave upon wave of the sickness swept over him and he fought desperately against the impulse to call out for help. He imagined the surprise on their faces as they assisted him, and then, afterward, the polite pretense that nothing had happened.

Why couldn't they leave him on Terra, doing the things he wanted to do—the things he could do well? He was an alien here. He had been an alien in the Service from the beginning. The agonizing days at the strato-school on Mars still stood vividly in his memory.

They had expected such great things of him. After all, he was the son of Commandant Jemson and his brother Ken had been one of the most brilliant graduates the school ever had. Now, young Dirk was there to carry on in the Jemson tradition—to make good for the Commandant and for the gallant Ken who had lost his life in the first attempt made to land on Setebos.

THEY had expected great things—but they had been disappointed. Of course, his panic on the trip to Mars had been understandable. The first experience in space. It often happened so. Soon he'd be as calm and unaffected as the others.

Then, there had been the practice flight to Deimos. For Dirk, it still had the immediacy of a nightmare. It was five years now—more than five—and yet he could still visualize the cramped quarters of that training ship.

The instructor had been a fish-faced young man named Petley. Ensign Petley. He had seen in Dirk Jemson a chance for advancement. Give the commandant's son the breaks, he had told himself, and you'll get a promotion.

As the trainer approached Deimos, Petley had turned from the visi-shield and smiled patronizingly at the tensed class who crowded around him.

"We're approaching Deimos, class," he said, and his lips made little smacking noises as he spoke. "I'm going to let Dirk show us how to make a landing. Dirk — take the controls."

And with that, he had gestured to Dirk and stepped back. The silence in the training ship had been absolute. The other thirteen in the class stared at the recipient of this signal honor. Who but the son of the commandant would be trusted to land a ship on his first training flight? Who but the heir to the space-mantle of Commandant Jemson.

Dirk remembered the sticky perspiration that had drenched his uniform as he had stared in disbelief at the beaming Petley. He had stammered some excuse, but Petley had smiled and firmly insisted. This was no time to be modest.

Dirk had closed his eyes, moved to the controls. Through the visi-shield, the grey orb of Deimos rushed toward him. The black maw of space was a swirling, twisting, rotating nightmare that blurred up at him.

In the background, Ensign Petley had murmured explanations to the watchers. Closer and closer whirled Deimos. Dirk's hands had faltered over the degravitator. Somehow, the movement of the universe had communicated itself to him. His mind, his heart, his stomach all swam in a whirlpool of black motion.

"Now, Dirk!" Petley's voice was sharp. "Now! Show the class!"

The eyes had been on him—the urgency in the voice had been great—but the hypnotic spinning of Deimos in the visi-shield was irresistible. With a little sigh, Dirk had blacked out.

There had been very little said, naturally. Petley had broken the rules in turning a ship over to a boot, in the first place; and one of the other trainees had saved them by seizing the controls at the crucial moment and decelerating. Dirk had asked to be transferred to another class, and his request was granted. He was, after all, the Commandant's son and allowances must be made.

Enough allowances were made to permit him to graduate from the strato-school. He was a great theorist, his instructors agreed. Perhaps he lacked a little of his father's daring and drive, but he had the same comprehension, the same inter-stellar grasp.

And after graduation, nothing sensational. A little routine work between Mars and Luna — work which permitted him to stay in the navigator's cell — away from the visi-shield—away from the twisting whirlpool of space.

For, after all, promotions must not come too rapidly. He was the son of a famous man and sons of famous men are closely observed by the Universe. When he rose, it must not be the result of family, but because he was well qualified and experienced.

HIS days as a Lunar navigator were as happy as any Dirk had known, but they were not to last. Commandant Jemson was planning another voyage of exploration—the most audacious in his long and brilliant career. The goal was the dark satellite known as Caliban. A space armada would accompany the commandant on this, the climactic space-trek of his colorful career, and in charge of one cruiser in the fleet would be Dirk Jemson—the commandant's brilliant but untried son.

And now, they were approaching Caliban.

"What d'ya think we'll find on Caliban, Doc?" Kennedy addressed his question to Tabor, who had closed his book with a little sigh, and was staring dreamily ahead.

"Very little." Tabor pursed his lips in an academic pout. "It is my theory that the atmosphere on Caliban will not support organic life as we know it."

"But there could be other kinds? Like the Venusians, maybe, or those things from Circe I've seen at the Zoo."

Tabor nodded. "That's what makes being a part of this expedition so stimulating. When we reach Caliban, I will be the first biophysicist to be permitted to examine the satellite. I'll be the first to coordinate fact and theory."

Allen peered through the visishield. "You can start coordinatin' pretty soon, Doc. Caliban's just ahead."

As Allen spoke, the audio-visor above his head hummed and flickered. Dirk tensed himself. This was it. In a few seconds, that humming and flickering would materialize and he would be watching his father's face, hearing his father's voice.

As with a single impulse, the other three men in the cabin turned and regarded Dirk. They seemed to sense that the moment was his. Allen stepped back from the visishield; Kennedy turned from his gauges.

Commandant Jemson's face spread on the screen like a slow stain. He cleared his voice. This was a strong face. The eyes were compelling; the nose generous and the mouth firm. Steel grey hair, cut short, completed the impression of controlled power.

"Attention," the voice said; and it, too, was dynamic, forceful. "Attention, all participants in Operation Caliban. We are now approaching our objective. The flight, thus far, has been distinguished by its orderliness. We know that the landing will be equally well-organized. The high command has decided that the space-cruiser ICARUS, piloted by Lieutenant Dirk Jemson, shall have the honor of leading the armada in. If that is clear, we will rendezvous on Caliban."

The image flickered for a moment and then dwindled away. The die was cast. Shakily, Dirk rose to his feet. There had been a second when he had harbored the wild hope that his father might reserve the honor of the first landing for himself; that hope had foundered and gone down. The echo of the older man's pride hung suspended in Dirk's mind. Why couldn't the commandant understand that with Dirk it was different? Why couldn't he see the difference?

"Are you all right, sir?" That was Allen, struggling to mask his concern with an air of forced casualness.

"Yes." Dirk's voice sounded strained and taut. "Yes. I'm all right. I'll take over, Allen." He moved toward the visi-shield, and

Allen retreated.

They were staring at him now, as those fellow students had stared long years before; but now, it was Caliban which bobbed in the visi-shield, not Deimos; this was the lead ship in the Jemson Armada, not a trainer; they were all waiting for him—Dirk Jemson—the commandant's son—to lead them in.

HE clutched at the controls. His mouth was dry and his eyes ached. He longed desperately to close them—to shut out the spinning universe before him. He stared at his hands on the controls and they seemed detached—as if they belonged to someone else.

Allen was at his shoulder with a suggestive clearing of his throat: "Are you sure, lieutenant, that you're well?"

Impatiently, Dirk nodded. Why didn't they leave him alone? Why couldn't they ALL leave him alone?

The audio-visor hummed. "We're waiting, ICARUS. Go ahead."

They were waiting. Waiting on him. This was the moment—the moment he had hoped to avoid—when other men depended on him to put them into a safe harbor in space. His father was testing him. He was supposed to show the superiority of the breed—the special gifts that made the Jemsons men apart.

He closed his eyes for a moment and began to decelerate.

"Careful of the flagship!" Kennedy's voice was low, but tense. "You're cutting in on him."

Dirk forced himself to open his eyes. The universe spun and whirled in a confused circle before him and in the center of that gyrating mass was the flagship. Somehow he missed it.

"Steady on your course, ICARUS!" This was the crisp instruction on the audio-visor.

Caliban rushed toward them, but all space between was a twisting, writhing spectrum of color. Dirk's mind was a pinwheel, spinning in reckless abandon toward oblivion. He couldn't keep his eyes open. He was sick. Really sick. A sob tore through his clenched teeth. He slumped over the controls.

"Lieutenant!" That was Allen's voice, and then, something shoved him to the floor. There was a wrenching, tearing of metal, and a sickening lurch. Resolutely, Dirk kept his eyes tight shut against what he might see when he opened them.

There was a murmur of voices—Kennedy, Allen, Tabor—and then, gradually, a deceleration as the ship settled into Caliban's atmosphere.

It had happened again—only not in an isolated training ship with a fish-faced instructor, but before the entire Armada. They all knew now, and Dirk was almost relieved. It was as if he had relinquished a role that he had been ill-suited to play.

"Lieutenant Jemson," a voice said close to his ear. "Lieutenant are you all right?" It was Tabor, the biophysicist.

Dirk opened his eyes. Allen and Kennedy were at the controls. The cruiser was settling on its tail for a landing. Tabor's face was a study in embarrassed concern.

Dirk nodded. He must say something. "Sure. Sure. I'm all right. Anyone else hurt?"

Tabor shook his head. "We sheared a fin off the flagship, but no one was injured. What happened to you?"

Dirk closed his eyes again. What answer could he give? "Just space dizziness", he said. "That's all. Space dizziness." He looked to catch Tabor's reaction.

The scientist nodded, but behind his eyes was a puzzlement. Space dizziness in a lieutenant of the Federation's space armada? Space dizziness in the son of Commandant Jemson?

"All clear." Allen and Kennedy were scrupulously avoiding his eyes, busying themselves with the reports and logs.

Suddenly, he wished that he could make them understand. He wished that there were words which would communicate to them the sinking feeling that had seized him as he gazed into the visi-shield. But there were no words. These were men innured to space. They could not appreciate the shattering malady that gripped him.

TABOR rose and moved over to the others. They conversed quietly, and once or twice, Dirk saw them nod in his direction. Then he closed his eyes again. It was better that way. Soon enough he would have to face his father. And what could be said? There were no excuses. He had failed. If Allen had not been quick, the ICARUS would have been lost; perhaps the entire Armada jeopardized. No. There was no excuse.

And he could expect no forgiveness. If it was difficult for these men now with him to understand his weakness, it would be impossible for his father. Why couldn't Ken have lived, he wondered. He was the son the Commandant wanted. He had the dash and the spirit. He was never troubled by consequences. He acted on impulse . . . bravely, daringly.

The trio was donning space suits, preparing to venture out onto Caliban. He half-raised himself.

"Going with us, lieutenant?" Allen asked the question for the others.

Dirk hesitated and Kennedy interposed: "Maybe you'd rather have us send a Med over to take care of you."

The lieutenant shook his head tiredly. "I'll be all right. Thanks."

They turned away in relief and zipped on the space uniforms. Just as they were preparing to enter the compression chamber, the audio-visor hummed. They paused and looked back expectantly.

The sleek face of the commandant's orderly blurred into focus. "Lieutenant Jemson will report to the commandant aboard the flagship." That was all. The picture faded.

Instinctively, the trio in the doorway looked toward Dick. He managed a smile and waved them on. After a moment's hesitation, they stepped into the compression chamber and out of sight.

With fumbling hands, he put on his own space suit. What would his father say? What could he say? Words would only make it worse. And Commandant Jemson was not a man to seek out the kind word, the gentle phrase. His speech resembled his tactics—raw, direct, uncompromising.

Slowly, Dirk moved into the compression chamber and from it into the murk of the world known as Caliban. Even protected as he was by his space suit, Dirk could sense the slimy chill in the atmosphere. It was as if wet, fibrous hands pushed at his suit; as if oozing tendrils slithered across his visor plate. The footing was insecure as well, and he had the unpleasant sensation that he was walking on raw eggs.

Dark Caliban, he thought, pushing his way through the grey-brown fog. Dark Caliban—scene of Dirk Jemson's final shame and disgrace. Poor dad. This was to have been his crowning achievement and all it had been was a blow to his pride.

Impatiently, Dirk swiped at his glass visor plate with his swathed hands. Some substance—gelatinous and moist—seemed to have formed there.

The guard at the flagship was expecting him, and he quickly entered the compression chamber and doffed the uniform. As he put it on a hook to await his return, he noticed with a little shudder of revulsion that the jelly-like things he had noticed on his visor were also clustered here and there in the folds of his space suit. This was probably the life to which Tabor had referred.

The orderly outside his father's office saluted, but Dirk thought he sensed in the click of the heels, the tilt of the chin just a nuance of disrespect—as an executioner might salute the criminal just before the disintegrating switch were thrown.

COMMANDANT Jemson was seated at an enormous table of batek wood from Thule. He didn't look up when Dirk closed the cabin door behind him and waited at attention.

The Commandant was not a large man, yet he managed somehow through the sheer force of his personality to convey the impression of a giant. Seated now behind the great table, he seemed some remote demi-god, omnipotent and untouchable.

Just as Dirk was about to clear his throat to ease the tension, his father spoke: "Come to the table." That was all. The voice was carefully modulated and controlled. Too carefully.

Dirk was face to face with his father across the glistening batekwood. Looking down into its polished surface, he could see his own white face, as well as each movement of his father's hands.

"You disgraced me."

The three words were thrown at him with electric force. Never before in his life could Dirk remember hearing three words spoken with such intensity and emotion. All of his father's life was summed up in that anguished declaration; all the hopes that had been sabotaged; all the dreams that were now derelict; and yet, the three words were spoken so quietly, they scarcely carried across the room.

He wished his father would look up at him. If he could see the eyes, it might be easier. "You shouldn't have expected me to do it. You had no right to expect it of me."

"No right!" The Commandant stood abruptly, his knuckles white against the wood of the table as he leaned forward. "What do you think I had left in my life but you—and the things you might do? What do you think I built my world on after Ken was killed? No right!" The eyes raked him now with a barrage of contempt and hurt. "You would have killed those men. Killed them because you're a weakling! A coward!"

The words fell in the silent room like coiling snakes. Dirk stepped back. The hate, frustration and disappointment which radiated from the older man was almost unbearable. "You can't understand, dad," he faltered.

"No. I can't. And don't call me 'dad.' You're no longer my son. No Jemson could put the lives of his men in jeopardy, no matter how stricken he might be. And this isn't the first time. I've closed my eyes. I told myself you were young; that you'd grow into this as you matured."

"You shouldn't have tried to make me a space pilot. It's not for me. I could have found some other life on Terra . . . something that I could have done well . . . could have made you proud."

"Proud!" The square shoulders sagged, and the old man sank down into his chair. "Proud. Proud of a weakling who puts his own comfort above the lives of his crew?" He stared again at the polished table surface, as if he might read there an answer to the dilemma. "If I hadn't seen it, I wouldn't have believed it."

"Not all men are alike, dad. You

must see that." But Dirk knew it was hopeless. His father knew only one life and that his son could want another was beyond his comprehension.

"You'll never have a chance to fail anyone else."

"What do you mean?"

The Commandant pushed a parchment across the table. "Your discharge. Dishonorable. You'll return to Terra at once. They're fueling a small ship for you now. You'll have to manage it alone. I can't spare anyone to pilot it for you."

Dirk picked up the parchment with a trembling hand. "Dad, we can't separate like this. I'm sorry I failed you. You just gave me a job that was too big for me."

There was a pause, and when the commandant spoke again, it was in a voice so low that Dirk could scarcely hear him. "What I've done, I did, not for myself, but for my sons. What fame I've won, I didn't seek selfishly, but only in order that my sons might inherit a name for honor, for courage, for integrity. I've devoted a lifetime to establishing a name to pass on to my sons . . . a name the Universe could speak with pride." The strong voice broke. The Commandant raised his eyes and regarded Dirk. "I've wasted my life building something for my sons. Wasted it, because both my sons are DEAD!"

"Dad!" Dirk's voice snapped in the quiet room like a whip.

"Lieutenant, you are dismissed." The commandant regarded the table top.

"Listen to me! Please!" Dirk leaned across the table. "I know what it's meant to you, dad, but I can't help myself. You've got to believe that I've tried. All these years, I've tried to be what you wanted . . . what you thought I was . . . but it's hopeless."

"I said you were dismissed, lieutenant. Take off for Terra as soon as your ship is fueled."

Dirk stood staring in disbelief at his father for a long moment, and then, he turned and walked slowly to the door. He paused with his hand on the latch. "I'm sorry, dad," he said, and turning swiftly, went out of the room.

THE flagship was strangely quiet as he walked down the passageway to the compression chamber. It was as if the entire crew mourned with the commandant the passing of his son. *"You disgraced me. You disgraced me. You disgraced me."* The phrase whirled and circled in his mind.

The guard outside the compression chamber stood stiffly at attention as Dirk approached. Looking at the impassive young face, Dirk felt a sudden twist of envy. Here was a man happy in his chosen duties, working out his destiny in an honorable and satisfying way.

Inside the chamber, Dirk began automatically to put on his space suit. What possible future could there be for him on Terra? If he changed his name, perhaps he could find a little happiness; but could he ever erase the picture in his mind of his father's face, or the sound of a low voice ceaselessly repeating "You disgraced me."?

On the floor beneath the peg on which he had hung his space suit, he noticed a puddle of ooze—the colorless gelatine he had seen on his visor. Was his imagination working overtime, or was there more of it now than when he had gone in to talk to his father? It couldn't be, and yet he had thought there were only a few blotches of it on his suit.

The world of Caliban was always in half-darkness. Dirk found this somehow comforting as he pushed through the murk to the command center. He actually felt less alien here than on sunlit Terra.

His father had already taken action, he learned from the officer in charge. A small SD-4 reconnaissance ship had been placed at his disposal. It was fueled and he could blast off whenever he chose. The officer avoided his eyes, Dirk noted, and there was between the two of them, an elaborate pretense that nothing had happened.

With his orders, Dirk returned to the ICARUS for his gear. He hoped that the others would not have returned, but he was disappointed. Tabor was in the cruiser when he stepped aboard. The biophysicist was crouched over his microscope, concentrating intently on some specimen he had found. He was scarcely aware that Dirk had come in.

There weren't many things to collect. An officer in the Space Armada learned to travel light. He didn't hurry. He was reluctant to leave the ICARUS, to isolate himself in the cramped quarters of the SD-4, to leave behind forever the life which he had tried to take as his own.

Tabor huddled over his microscope, punctuating the silence with little exclamations of surprise. The specimen on the slide was apparently proving of interest. Another happy man, thought Dirk.

He hesitated in the doorway and looked back. "Good-bye, Tabor."

The man at the microscope only half-turned. "This is the most amazing cell I've ever examined. Incredible. Apparently it's the effect of oxygen on the organism. What a sensational announcement this will be on Terra. Sensational."

Dirk nodded at Tabor's back. Why should he have thought the scientist would be interested in his going? He was just another space officer washing out. Wearily, he donned his space suit once more. The gelatine was everywhere. An expanding pool of it stood in the compression chamber. Idly, he wondered if it could be the specimen causing Tabor's excitement.

Parties were already out combing Caliban. This would be another triumph for Commandant Jemson; another glorious achievement for the Grand Old Man of Space. The reports need carry no mention of the disgrace and shame of a lieutenant in the commandant's armada — an ex-lieutenant whose name also happened to be Jemson.

DIRK stopped beside the trim little SD-4. What if he went back to his father—if he begged for another chance—a chance to prove that he WAS a Jemson worthy of the name. The answer was there in the crawling dark of Caliban. There was no second chance. His father had made a decision.

Slipping out of his space suit in the narrow confines of the little reconnaissance ship, Dirk noticed that the omnipresent grey ooze had clung to his suit and boots. It lay in quivering globules on the floor.

Automatically, he checked his controls and got a clearance from the command center. The take-off was uneventful, and with the speed of light, he slipped through the atmosphere of Caliban and into the whirling void of space.

Quickly, he made his calculations and set his course for Terra. No margin for error in an SD-4. The fuel tank held only enough for the one-way trip to Terra. Any miscalculation might prove fatal.

Once set, however, the controls were fool-proof. He could relax, forget the spinning galaxies around him, forget that he was a lost mote in the infinite void. He could close his eyes and forget the last twenty-four hours, or even the last twenty-four years, for after all, the error over Caliban was only the climax of his many years of maladjustment.

His father would be all right. He would still have his beloved armada, and there would always be new worlds to conquer; until after one such expedition, the commandant would fail to return; and that was the way he'd want it. Yes. His father was all right. His life was too solidly based to be shaken.

But what of himself? What lay ahead for him on Terra? A space-pilot with a dishonorable discharge!

. . . For some time, he had experienced a growing sensation that he was being observed, that someone or something was behind him, watching. He closed his eyes. Space nerves. That's all it was. There was no one else in the SD-4. He was alone. And yet, the feeling persisted. He felt the small hairs on the back of his neck stand on end, and a cold shiver shook him. He had to turn around. He couldn't resist the impulse. Slowly, he opened his eyes and swiveled in his chair.

The floor in the corner where he

had hung his space suit was alive! A spreading, pulsating jelly . . . quivering in the half-light of the cabin. This was a living thing — growing.

For a moment, all he could do was sit and stare in hypnotic horror at the tremelloid monstrosity quaking in the corner. Even as he watched, another section of the floor was obscured by the viscous transparency.

He crouched against the instrument panel and drew his disinteray. Fighting down the sick panic that swelled in his throat, he fired, time after time, into the undulating, pulpy mass on the floor. The impact had no visible effect. Still he could see it growing . . . spilling with soft, slobbery noises across the ship toward him.

Frantically, he threw up a temporary barricade between himself and the Thing: some filing cabinets, a desk, an up-ended chair. Perhaps that would check its terrible, oozing progress for a little while.

AT the instrument panel, he checked his position. With a little luck, he might reach Terra before the thing got through to him. It depended on how rapidly it was growing. As he strained to hear, a sort of sucking sound came from it now as it worked behind the barricade.

His audio-visor suddenly flickered and hummed. Who would be calling him? Only someone on Caliban. His father? But why? Unless . . .

The face rippled onto the screen. His father's face—but it seemed that the face had aged twenty years since the interview short hours before.

"Dirk," the voice said. "Dirk—have you checked your ship?"

He pushed the talk-back. "Yes, dad. There's something . . . something that looks like jelly. It's growing. The disinteray doesn't stop it."

"You've got to turn back, Dirk. Nothing will stop that jelly-thing. As long as it gets oxygen, it'll keep growing! You've got to turn back to Caliban."

Dirk's eyes flickered to the gauges on the panel. "There's not enough fuel to get me back to Caliban. I can feel the pull of Terra's solar system already."

The visor went abruptly blank and then Tabor's face replaced his father's on the screen. "Listen to me, Dirk," Tabor said, and the academic hesitancy had been discarded for a terrible urgency. "That stuff in your ship is wild cells. They're the only life on Caliban. Oxygen has a peculiar effect on them. Makes them multiply by geometric progression. Do you understand that?"

"I understand." Dirk's voice was a thing remote from him, apart.

"There's nothing you can do to

stop that growth. The disinteray won't help. You've got to get it back to Caliban—out of oxygen."

"I can't. I haven't enough fuel, Tabor." Dirk fought to keep his voice controlled and calm, but he could see already a crystalline ooze seeping under the desk, the filing cabinet. It couldn't be stopped.

"Can you reach Terra?" Tabor's face was knit into a perplexed maze of wrinkles.

"I might, if the thing doesn't grow too fast."

Tabor nodded. "If you get through to Terra, you'll live a little longer at least."

"What do you mean — a little longer?"

Tabor's face seemed to fill the screen and his eyes caught and held Dirk. "Don't you see? Even if you get out of the ship on Terra, the thing will follow. There'll be no stopping it. Eventually, it will engulf the whole earth."

"No!" Dirk's voice was a hoarse whisper. "No!"

"There will be nothing to stop it there. It will have all the oxygen it needs. I didn't know you were taking off. I'd have warned you. It's my fault." Tabor's voice trailed away and again the visor went blank.

"No," Dirk said softly. "It's my fault. All my fault. Not only have I failed dad, but now I'm going to destroy Terra." He stared at the slime as it inched with increasing speed across the cabin. The sucking, bubbling noise was quite clear now.

WITH an effort, Dirk pulled his eyes away from the Thing and looked through the visi-shield. Dead ahead lay the disc that was Terra—his home—a chance at life. To the left was the glimmering white brilliance of the sun.

"Dirk, The Commandant's face blurred back on the audio-visor. "Dirk, are you sure you can't get back here? Can't you try?"

"I know I can't," Dirk answered, and his tongue seemed to cling to the roof of his mouth.

"Maybe you can hit a spot on Terra that isn't thickly populated. Maybe they'll be able to devise some way of stopping it." The Commandant's voice sounded lame, strained.

For a moment, Dirk was unaware of his father's face on the audio-visor, unaware of the sucking mass that crept closer and closer to him, unaware of the swirling universe outside.

Dirk remembered only the spring green of the low, rolling hills around his home; the smell of lilacs battered by April rains; the cry of fledgling birds in the pink-grey of summer dawns; the crisp sound of snow under sled runners; and the gentle caress of water in a blue-green lake. Dirk remembered these things, and abruptlv. he changed his course.

"What are you doing?" His father checked him from the audio-visor. "You've changed your course. You're headed for the sun, Dirk!"

"I can't land on Terra, dad. You heard Tabor. I can't destroy Terra to save my own skin." He looked down at his shoes. The first jellied tentacle had slipped over his foot. With a wild kick, he threw it off. The floor was almost covered now, and it was rising on the walls. By geometric progression Tabor had said. It would go rapidly toward the end.

"You're going to crash into the sun. You're going to destroy the Thing, Dirk." His father's voice was hoarse. "If only there was something I could do to help!"

Dirk turned and looked full in his father's face. "There's nothing, dad. And I . . . I think it would be better if . . . if you didn't look any more. I'll smash the audio-visor." He raised the butt of his disinteray.

"Son. Wait." His father's voice stopped him as surely as if he had restrained him with his hand. "Son, I said some terrible things to you. I can only beg you to forgive me."

"I knew, dad. I understand."

The voice rumbled on, and tears formed in the steely eyes. "I beg you to forgive me. You're the bravest of the Jemsons, Dirk. The bravest. I'm proud of you, son. Understand? Proud of you."

Dirk managed a nod. The gelatine lapped now over the top of the desk. The ship was filled with the terrible sucking, bubbling noise.

Then with the butt of his disinteray, he smashed the audio-visor. He was alone; alone with the horror that inched toward him.

He concentrated on the visishield. The disc of Terra was plainer now, but safely to his right. Ahead lay the blazing furnace of the sun.

Dirk braced himself and waited. He tried not to think of the smothering ooze which crept slowly up to possess him. Instead, he thought of the purifying, purging white heat of the sun toward which they plunged; he thought of the sound of his father's voice saying: "I'm proud of you, son. I'm proud of you."

Dirk closed his eyes and smiled.

THE END

RIGHT AT THE TOP!

Dear Mr. Palmer:

As an ardent science fiction reader may I say that your new magazine is tops! I thought that you couldn't possibly turn out a finer magazine than OTHER WORLDS, but it seems that I was wrong.

IMAGINATION, with its first issue, is right there at the top. May I say that as a rule I only read one or two stories from each magazine I buy because I really don't have the time to sit down and read all of them. Naturally it's the short stories that I read first because of this. But when OW and IMAGINATION found their way into my home I found myself reading every page—even reading some of them over again! I must even admit to reading your editorial, and this is one item I avoid in most magazines. I truly enjoyed yours.

I will not attempt to rate the stories in your first issue (as so many fans do), except to say that they were all very good. Personally I do not approve of fans rating stories or even writing and saying that one or another was lousy. For it seems to me that opinions will be evenly divided on such ratings—five letters may say a story is terrific and five may say it's terrible. And after it's all boiled down, what good does it do? On the other hand, if you print bad stories consistently (and I know you never will!) you should be reminded, but in that case your circulation would tell the story.

So now that I've more or less told off the fans (help!) I hope the letters you publish will be an improvement over the general run of the field. As far as the magazine itself goes, I don't think you can improve it to any great extent—it's good already!

However, I would like to suggest one little thing if I may. When you print a novel like LOOK TO THE STARS (30,000) there should be one or more interior illos to go along with it. It kind of adds a little something to the story to find an occasional illo on the inside.

I like your policy of giving the word count after each story on the contents page. It gives the reader who must budget his time a chance to read the proper length yarn at the moment. (I realize there are some fans who read an entire issue at one sitting!)

(*Continued on Page* 160)

(*Continued from Page* 158)

I'll conclude my comments on your first issue by saying sincerely that I like your editing, your stories, your editorials, your reader's page, your illos—and everything else! Just keep the issues coming!

Yvonne K. Worth
1110 N. Cooper Ave.
Colorado Springs, Colo.

Thanks for the nice letter, Yvonne. As to rating the stories, it's true that opinions differ on each yarn, but really, we like to see ratings. That way we can get an overall picture of just what story was liked by the majority of the readers—and it's the majority we always want to please! Of course, when you tell us they were all very good, then all we can do is look proud and say: "Thanks a lot!" . . . Your suggestion on adding one or more interior illos to a long length story is a sound one. We'll remember that for future issues. And incidentally, all you other fans, if you have any suggestions to make for improving IMAGINATION, don't hesitate to let us know what they are. Ok? . . . Rap.

NEVILLE AND BRADBURY . .

Dear Mr. Palmer:

Congratulations on the launching of your new magazine, IMAGINATION. In the past year we fans have seen a large number of new magazines, but this is the most promising of the field. One can't judge a first issue too harshly, but I found the stories in this first issue somewhat disappointing. While they were better than those in the early issues of OTHER WORLDS, your sister publication, they were below the standard of the current OW.

Despite this, IMAGINATION has an indefinable "class" which OTHER WORLDS does not have. From the title through the Bok cover, the different type face, and through the illustrations, IMAGINATION seems to stress the more dignified aspects of science fiction while playing down the lurid or sensational. Only two other magazines, ASTOUNDING, and THE MAGAZINE OF FANTASY AND SCIENCE FICTION share this quality with you.

I presume that fantasy will be stressed in this magazine as compared with OTHER WORLDS, which will probably play up science fiction. This is fine, but I would like to put in a request for the gentle, humorous type of fantasy featured in the old UNKNOWN as compared with the lugubrious wordy stuff we are offered in most of the other fantasy magazines.

No Merritt imitators, please. Some styles can be imitated, some can't. Whether by Kuttner, Geier, or any of the others, I've never read a Merritt imitation which didn't have a leaden quality to it.

Perhaps LOOK TO THE STARS was the best in the first issue. Is Willard Hawkins a pen-name? The only other story I'll comment on here is WIND IN HER HAIR. I was rather surprised to see Ackerman comparing Neville to Bradbury. I understood after I read the story. The plot is not new—I was even able to predict the ending and the possible reasons after the title and the first few paragraphs. But Neville is the best, so far, of the Bradbury imitators. He's so good at it, in fact, that I was halfway through before I realized he was copying Ray's style. He managed to capture the Bradbury impact of hungry emotion without using Bradbury's most obvious trick of word repetition. Not being completely original, the Neville stories will probably never be literature as will the best of Bradbury's work. From the story and plot standpoint, however, Neville's yarns (WIND IN HER HAIR included) are better constructed than most Bradbury stories. By all means have Neville turn out more of this type for you. I think he has found the formula for success. Ordinarily I deplore imitations of writing styles. But in all fairness, Neville's story cannot be classed as a strict imitation of style. It's almost as good as the real thing. More, please!

Vernon L. McCain
R.F.D. No. 3
Nampa, Idaho

This business of "imitating" and "copying" of styles has come up in fan discussion columns for a long time. We'd like to add our own observations as long as the subject is open again. As far as the Neville story is concerned, we frankly don't see any connection between it and any Ray Bradbury "style." Bradbury, as far as style is concerned, is in much the same class as Thorne Smith. He has a style all his own. The Neville story was written simply, and with what we feel was a certain delicate beauty—which gave the story a solid dramatic impact. It, as far as we are concerned, cannot be called an imitation of Bradbury's style. We have heard many professional writers discussing various authors and their individual styles, and the observation has been made a number of times that Bradbury possesses a — for want of a better term—neurotic writing style. Some of his phrases—similes, etc., don't make sense in the conventional manner. (We recall offhand one phrase from a Bradbury story in WEIRD TALES: "Go pin your heart on the wall like a dripping medal.") There are many examples of this "style" which has made Bradbury what he is, but we don't think that Neville has attempted to adopt or imitate him in any manner. And we don't mean to say here that we don't like Bradbury! Heck, you've seen his work in our sister mag, OW, haven't you? And in all likelihood you'll see his work in IMAGINATION in the future.

We think that too much stress is put on "style stealing" these days. Actually, when you get right down to it, each author has his own way of expressing things—and it sometimes seems as if styles cross. At any rate, we're glad you want to see more of Neville's work. We do too!

As to Willard Hawkins, no, it is not a pen-name. As to the type of story IMAGINATION will feature—it will be equally as much science fiction as fantasy. And you ask for humorous fantasy—how about some of the yarns in this issue? Let us know what you think of Hal Annas, Milton Lesser, and Day Keene. . . . Rap.

A GREAT FIRST ISSUE

Dear Rap:

The first issue of IMAGINATION is great! That cover by Bok was really different. It was better than any other I've seen. Let's have some more by him!

WIND IN HER HAIR by Kris Neville was every word as good a story as you predicted in your editorial. And as to the general tone of the magazine, I'm glad to see no BEM's.—Just good stories about people in times to come. The story by Rog Phillips is one of my favorites.

But now I want to mention the two stories that really hit me. I'm speaking of THE SOUL STEALERS by Chet Geier, and LOOK TO THE STARS, by Willard Hawkins. While the rest of the issue was better than anything I've read in AMAZING, or others, these last two are two of the best yarns I've ever read. All I can ask is that you give us more like them in the future.

Oh, yes, before signing off for now, I'd like to say that I'm looking for pen-pals. Anybody interested?

David Rike
Box 203
Rodeo, Cal.

Good enough, Dave, you'll be seeing more stories of the kind you like. . . . And we'd only like to add here that the Reader's Section would have been much larger except that the second issue had to get to press early and we just didn't have time to include other letters. But from now on you'll find a larger Reader's Section—so just get your letters in as early as possible! . . . Rap.

AND WHAT A FUTURE!

Dear Rap:

Several times I've been tempted to write letters of commendation or otherwise to a science fiction magazine, but it took the first issue of IMAGINATION to spur me into action. Now I just sit here with the first issue of you-know-what before me, and what happens—I'm speechless! But what could be expected? It isn't often one can open a magazine and find each story so engrossing that he doesn't know where to start!

And what stories! After a great deal of scientific calculation, the ratings seem to come out like this:

1. LOOK TO THE STARS by Willard Hawkins. It wasn't hard to give that story first place!

2. WIND IN HER HAIR by Kris Neville.

3. INHERITANCE by Edward W. Ludwig.

4. THE SOUL STEALERS by Chester Geier.

5. ONE FOR THE ROBOT — TWO FOR THE SAME by Rog Phillips.

I hate to do that to Rog—I like his stuff! OFTR—TFTS might grab top honors in another magazine—but not IMAGINATION!

But regardless of the general excellence of the magazine, what would have sold it to me in any case was the featuring of ROCKETSHIP X-M on the inside covers. Incidentally, Lisa's name was Van Horn, not Van Meter . . . And you say that ROCKETSHIP X-M is the second scientifilm Hollywood has produced, yet it has come out before DESTINATION MOON. How come?

I can only hope that October 1st will be an even greater day in science fiction than August 1st (when MADGE first appeared), and if I know you, Rap, it will be, if that is possible. May I add just four words to Forrie Ackerman's toast: "—And *WHAT* a future!"

Mary Jane Stewart
4075 N. Castle Ave.
Portland 12, Ore.

Your praise for "Madge" has us really bowled over, Mary Jane. All we hope is that we continue to please you—and all our readers. And you do know us—we certainly will try to make each on sale date a bigger event than the last one! Sorry for the slip on the Lisa Van Horn mention. . . . Rap.

Printed in U.S.A.

CAPTAIN FUTURE
WIZARD OF SCIENCE
COMET
FICTION AND FACT OF THE PRIZE-RING
FIGHT STORIES
THE BLACK UHLAN
HEADQUARTERS DETECTIVE
MASKED RIDER WESTERN
FIGHTING ACES OF WAR SKIES
WINGS
10 STORY WESTERN
ADVENTURE NOVELS
Thrilling Stories of the Sky Trails
AIR STORIES
THE NIGHT HAWK
FIGHTING DAREDEVILS OF TODAY'S WAR
AIR WAR
THE ALL-STORY
ARMY Romances
BASKETBALL STORIES
Battle Stories
O'LEARY IN ACTION IN ETHIOPIA
BLACK BOOK DETECTIVE
GOLDEN FLEECE
HIGH-SEAS ADVENTURES
THE SEA ROGUE
INDIAN Stories
BRIDE of the TOMAHAWK PACK
MY LIFE WITH SITTING BULL
LONE RANGER
MAGIC CARPET MAGAZINE
PEARLS FROM MACAO
MARVEL SCIENCE STORIES
NEW DETECTIVE
North-West ROMANCES
GIRL OF WHITE WATER TRAIL
Oriental Stories
PHANTOM DETECTIVE
PLANET stories
QUEEN OF THE MARTIAN CATACOMBS
POPULAR DETECTIVE
PRIVATE DETECTIVE
LOVE STORIES OF THE REAL WEST
RANCH ROMANCES
Maid of the Valley
RANGE RIDERS
SIX-GUN VALLEY
Vice Squad DETECTIVE
SECRET of the HOUSE of HORROR
TOP-NOTCH STORIES ... TOP-NOTCH WRITERS
UNDERWORLD DETECTIVE
KILLER BAIT
THRILLING WONDER STORIES
THE FEDERALS IN ACTION
G-MEN
GIVE 'EM HELL
SCIENCE FICTION
SPICY-ADVENTURE STORIES
HELL'S RIVER

www.ingramcontent.com/pod-product-compliance
Lightning Source LLC
LaVergne TN
LVHW090953080826
845145LV00003B/988